A Dangerous Business

SCOTTISH WEREBEARS BOOK 2

LORELEI MOONE

CONTENTS

CHAPTER ONE

All was not well in Rannoch, Scotland. Heidi Blackwood felt her heartbeat speed up, and the urge to protest grew ever stronger in her chest. *How the hell had this happened?*

"You may not like the idea of leaving, but we need one of our own inside the Alliance. You said so yourself," Eric Blackwood said while giving his daughter a strict look.

"Yeah, but..." *I never thought it would be me,* Heidi thought. Her father's news came as a bit of a shock. Whenever the topic of the Alliance had come up, Heidi had always expected one of the young males of the pack to be chosen as their representative to the Alliance. Never once did she think it could be her.

"I've made the necessary arrangements. You are to travel to Edinburgh and join them. I've spoken to their local leader, Jamie Abbott, already." Her dad sounded firm. He wouldn't be receptive to any arguments she would think of, and she didn't have anything sensible to add, either. She just needed a moment to let the information sink in.

Of course, he was right. They needed someone they could rely on to join the Alliance. Who could be more reliable than Heidi herself? She'd learned at an early age that if you wanted something done right, you had to do it yourself. It was time to put her money where her mouth was.

She took a deep breath and tried to focus.

"I'll pack my things." Heidi turned on her heel and headed out of the living room of the cozy log hut where she lived with her parents, and up the stairs to her bedroom.

It may have been years since she had been of age technically, but the Wolves of Rannoch didn't follow the same rules that human society did. She would be considered her father's daughter first of all and her own woman second, no matter how old she was. Only her marriage to an eligible wolf would change that, but Heidi had no intention of throwing herself into yet another situation where she'd be forced to dance to someone else's tune.

In a way this assignment was a blessing in disguise, Heidi thought. She wondered if her father had picked her because he'd sensed that she would soon outgrow Rannoch and its strict rules. Or perhaps it was simply because he trusted her more than the others. She wanted to think it was maybe a bit of both.

As she started throwing clothes and a few weapons into an overnight bag, she wondered what the other members of the Alliance would be like. Jamie Abbott was a bear, she already knew that.

The rivalry between bears and wolves was one of the main reasons her father had pushed for one of their own to join the Alliance in the first place, even though they'd had a truce between their species for the past few years. She'd heard whispers over campfires about other, more unusual species of shifters inside the Alliance, but couldn't be sure if those were just rumors. Bears and wolves, that was the most likely scenario.

She also wondered what it would be like to stay in Edinburgh. She'd visited the city a few times, but had never actually lived away from home. It could be exciting, an adventure, something a little different. But if Heidi was completely honest with herself, it was also a little scary.

Twenty-two years she'd spent in this room, in this house, safe in the knowledge that there was an entire pack surrounding her who would do anything to protect the alpha's daughter. Not that she'd needed protection – she was strong, taller than most of the other females her age, and broader as well. She was no pushover and had gotten into plenty of scraps growing up. She was used to winning, even when fighting some of the boys in her pack.

But the outside world was largely a mystery to Heidi. Bears, especially. She'd never even met one, though of course that would change shortly.

It didn't take her long to pack a few changes of clothes and a good selection of knives and other weaponry she thought might come in handy, but she spent much too long poring over all that *other stuff*. A photo album, her favorite books. She even found herself holding her old diary, which she hadn't written in for years but which now felt like too precious a thing to leave behind.

No, she was going to make a fresh start in Edinburgh. Plus, what would the other members of the Alliance say if they found all these girly mementos in her things? They wouldn't take her seriously, and she couldn't have that.

She hurriedly put all her old stuff into the top drawer of her dresser and zipped up the bag. She was ready.

A deep breath later, she picked up the bag and closed the door of her bedroom for what would be the last time in a good while. She had no idea when she would return, and did her best not to think of that too much.

Duty called. It was an honor that her father had picked her to represent them in the Alliance, and she would do her best to live up to his expectations.

Downstairs, beside her dad, Heidi's mom was waiting with her arms crossed. Clearly she was unhappy that Heidi was to leave, but she'd had no choice in the matter. An alpha's decision-making powers were absolute, even within the home.

"You just be careful, all right, darling?" Heidi's mom, Rebecca Blackwood, gave her a warm hug. Her voice betrayed the emotions welling up in her chest.

"I'll be fine, really," Heidi responded, trying to convince herself as well as her mom.

It was difficult not to be emotional, and all of a sudden, during this very rare embrace, it struck Heidi how much shorter and smaller her mom actually was. She felt fragile, sniffling slightly as she tried to keep the beginnings of tears in check.

"Call when you get there, promise me."

"Of course," Heidi forced a smile as she extricated herself from the continuing hug. Things were getting awkward now and if she didn't leave soon, she'd be crying puddles herself. It was important to Heidi to leave Rannoch with her head held high. No longer the little girl, but a she-wolf with an important job to do. An opportunity like this didn't come along every day.

Her dad cleared his throat and gave her a much more stoic, pat-on-the-back style hug when she approached him.

"Good girl. Do your job, follow orders, and do us proud. But always remember why you're there: in the end it's always us against them." He nodded at Heidi, and she thought she could see a little glimmer of something in his eyes as well. Pride? Worry? She wasn't quite sure what it was, but she knew she'd never seen it before.

"Yes, Dad." Although she couldn't guess what exactly was going on in her father's head, she understood his words perfectly. She was to make sure that the Alliance served the wolves as much as it did the bears and other species.

As long as it was humans against shifters, it would be

easy to pick sides, but if she found out that the Alliance was in any way favoring one of the other species over wolves, she had to make sure her father was notified. She had to be his eyes and ears inside the Alliance.

"Now be on your way, before you miss the train." Eric Blackwood nodded at Heidi one last time, signaling it really was time for her to leave.

So Heidi picked up her stuff, along with the few provisions her mom had packed, and headed straight out the door without looking back even once.

With her head held high, she marched towards the edge of the settlement, where one of the pack's jeeps was waiting. The drive was short and quiet – she didn't exchange a single word with the young wolf who was driving. Honestly, she was so lost in thought for most of it that she didn't even remember who it was.

The whole journey, including getting off at the station and waiting for her train to Edinburgh, passed in a blur. She had no idea what would be waiting for her, so her mind couldn't stop speculating about it.

Once in the train, she barely took note of the cloudy, rain-lashed countryside as it passed by at high speed outside the windows. Her attention was focused solely on the mobile phone in her hand, and the address and directions programmed into it. From the station, she'd take a bus, and a short walk later she'd arrive at the Alliance office.

What would it look like? A shiny modern affair, bustling with activity, dotted with fancy computer screens and complicated maps and things, like you see on detective shows? Or perhaps it was more of a secret lair type of place, hidden away in an old warehouse, complete with training facilities and a stockpile of weapons.

Heidi closed her eyes and tried to relax, forcing herself

to breathe more slowly. It would take a few more hours to get there, and somehow she was certain that she'd need all her energy then.

———•◆•———

When Heidi awoke, she had no idea how long she'd been asleep. The train was still mostly empty, only a few seats were taken in her carriage, and luckily nobody had sat anywhere near her. She didn't feel all that sociable.

At least her nap had helped her get her thoughts in order. She was on her own now, and she would manage. Somehow.

Not long after waking up did the scenery outside change as well. The lush green landscapes had made way for more built-up areas. They were getting close to the city. Village after village zipped past outside, and Heidi started recognizing some of the station names from her last trip to Edinburgh. Within twenty minutes, they pulled into their final destination and it was time to collect her stuff and disembark.

The bus ride also went seamlessly, even though she had been a bit worried about missing her stop. With the help of the phone, making her way to the Alliance address was equally easy.

After checking and double-checking that the house number matched what was in her phone, she finally knocked against the weather-beaten wood. A few flakes of faded blue paint chipped off and fell to the ground as she did so.

Despite her expectations being vague, the outside of the office didn't match up. It looked neither modern nor particularly mysterious. The building was old, in a downtrodden part of town, and plain ugly.

Would the inside be any better?

Finally, a short wait later, someone opened the door. Her disappointments about where she'd found herself vanished instantly and were replaced by utter shock and disbelief, along with something else. Something more intimate.

His scent hit her first. A mixture of clean laundry and unmistakably male hormones made its way into her nostrils, setting her insides alight with a need she'd never felt before. His fragrance was different, unlike any other wolf she'd ever met.

The confused sensations she felt reminded her of the stories she'd heard, about when a wolf finds his one true mate. And yet, she wasn't elated like most of her peers would have been, she was royally pissed off. She's been sent on this important mission, and the first thing that happens is she wants to mate with a coworker? *Unacceptable.*

Heidi couldn't quite make out what the man who had opened the door looked like, only that he was tall, so tall he blocked out most of the light from inside the room. Two amber eyes burned into her with such intensity that she wanted - but couldn't bring herself - to look away from them.

Damn. This was definitely the most inconvenient thing to happen to anyone, ever.

"Jamie gave me this address," Heidi heard herself say. "I'm Heidi."

CHAPTER TWO

Aidan McMillan shook his head, before focusing on Jamie Abbott's face again. "Just now, when we're starting to make progress, you want me to partner up with a rookie? You know I work better on my own."

"If the Alliance is to be successful in its campaign against the Sons of Domnall, we've got to keep growing. And it's not like you're in the middle of anything in particular right now," Jamie remarked.

Aidan glared at him, still incredulous over what he felt was a rash decision he should have been consulted about. But Jamie was the team leader, a role he took much too seriously indeed. *Team leader, but not a team player*, Aidan thought.

"You'll meet Heidi soon enough, don't worry. I'm sure you'll find her to be a valuable addition to the team. In the meantime, how are you getting on with that human you've been questioning?" Jamie crossed his arms and stared Aidan down until the latter finally backed down with a dejected sigh.

Involving a newbie was the wrong call. Aidan was certain of it but if he gave Jamie too much shit, he might stop being the laid-back leader and exact his revenge by turning into a micro-managing prick. That was something Aidan was keen to avoid, given how much of his day was spent on his private investigation, instead of the official one.

"The human, Alison, yes. She's given me a couple of websites to check out which at first glance appear to be just the usual racist, skinhead crap, but some of the wording used indicates they're speaking in code. They keep referring to themselves as 'the Sons', so that's promising. She's hiding something, I'm sure of it, but I think her information is sound."

"Good job, stay on that," Jamie said.

Aidan nodded. He'd already created a log-in on one of the sites, a discussion forum, and posted a fake introduction of himself. Although he wasn't sure how this group worked, he hoped that if he made all the right noises, perhaps someone would be in touch to find out if he'd want to be involved beyond just spewing hateful nonsense on the Internet.

"Right, well, I had better make a move." Jamie checked his watch, probably just to make a point, and put on his coat.

Edinburgh could get quite chilly this time of year and bears weren't so resistant to the cold while in human form. Shifting, of course, was completely out of the question in Scotland's second busiest city.

"Later," Aidan mumbled, as he watched Jamie leave the dingy office space they'd recently moved into. Then he folded himself into his much too small office chair and opened a browser window on the outdated desktop computer on his desk.

In addition to reading as many existing posts as he could on that skinhead website, he'd also been going through old articles about a certain event that had happened almost seventeen years ago to the day: the death of Aidan's parents. That's what he returned to.

He knew the words of most of them by heart already. Suspected car accidents on the far away Isle of Skye didn't get a lot of news coverage, so he'd been going through the same handful of articles again and again. Aidan felt like he was close to discovering something new in all that old information, but he wasn't quite sure if that was just because his frazzled brain was playing tricks on him.

Heidi, the rookie, Aidan scoffed to himself. Sure, he'd meet her, he'd force himself to be civil enough in person too, but no matter what Jamie and the Alliance wanted, his thoughts were still his own. A very dainty name for a girl joining a covert task force out to hunt shifter killers. Aidan could just imagine her: a fragile little thing who'd worry more about the state of her hair and nails than the mortal danger in which they may find themselves.

After reading the end of the Google search results about the accident, he logged onto the skinhead website again. To his pleasure, one of the most prolific members had already commented on his introductory post. The greeting was full of national-socialist symbolism, with a few marked differences.

Along with calling themselves "the Sons," the fact that they didn't refer to foreigners as much as "animals" or "monsters" signaled to Aidan that they weren't just ordinary skinheads. If only he could gain their trust somehow.

He browsed through the older discussions, adding to his existing notes about terminology to compile something of a glossary alongside other random observations he'd made. Every day he ended his shift with a quick read-through of all the new material, in an attempt to assimilate and learn about their "culture" to the point of it becoming second nature to him. There was no way of knowing if he'd need to apply it all someday soon, if he indeed managed to meet any of these people in person.

A knock on the door interrupted him. *Damn, was that her already?*

Aidan got up, his chair creaking loudly as though relieved to be rid of the burden. He quickly crossed the half dozen steps towards the door, and turned the heavy lock until it released with a loud click. He tried his best to force himself into a more neutral facial expression, but he'd always had a hard time keeping his emotional state under wraps.

As he pulled the door open, revealing a wind-blown female figure outside, he had even more trouble keeping himself in check.

The statuesque silhouette standing in front of the doorway was less dainty and a lot more Amazonian than his expectations had allowed for. Long strawberry blond hair blew in the wind and two eyes cut through the darkness, staring right at him. But none of that explained how he felt – not even her irresistibly sweet perfume could explain it. He was frozen in place, helpless and enchanted, his massive frame blocking the entire entrance.

"Mr. Abbott sent me here," she said, while shaking the odd fallen leaf off her coat. "I'm Heidi."

"Right," Aidan responded, barely.

"So..." She placed her hands on her hips and cocked her head to one side.

The pause that followed wasn't just awkward, it was painful.

"Are you going to introduce yourself, or...?"

Aidan had trouble focusing on her words, such was the immense pull her presence had on his inner bear. The beast was going crazy, fighting against his human side, desperate to break free and pounce on her.

"Oh, sorry. Aidan. Please come in." Though his feet felt like they were made of lead, Aidan stepped aside at last, allowing her into the office.

She eyed him suspiciously as she stepped inside and quickly pulled the door shut behind her.

They say there's nothing less flattering than fluorescent

light, but Aidan couldn't recall ever seeing a more radiant sight than the woman who stood in front of him now. Her strong build suggested she came from a healthy lineage. She was a fighter. Intelligent yet slightly hostile green eyes stared at him; clearly, she did not suffer fools kindly and was used to being in charge wherever she went.

"So you're the rookie," Aidan remarked, more to himself than to her.

She frowned and pressed her lips together to form a tight line. Yep, a dominant personality, this one – as beautiful as she was strong-willed. Although she looked younger than him in years, she was no girl, but all woman.

It didn't seem like it at the time, but Aidan was usually good with the opposite sex. He was a reasonably witty conversationalist, and could usually get a laugh or two out of even the most difficult audience. It certainly helped that his large, muscular frame meant that most women found him attractive as well.

All that was wiped away now. In front of Heidi, Aidan felt helplessly stupid, like anything that would come out of his mouth would be all wrong.

Work. He should play it cool and talk about work.

"Welcome. You can take that desk." Aidan pointed at the unused table set against the far wall of the office.

Their eyes met again. Hers looked strangely fiery, even if they were a cool shade of green, and distrustful.

"Thanks," she said, her intonation making it sound like a question rather than a statement. He observed her as she walked to the dust covered desk and placed her overnight bag down onto the ground beside it.

Her gait suggested she was strong, flexible, but even that coat couldn't disguise that she had curves in all the right places, especially around the hips. She certainly didn't seem fragile, which pleased Aidan's inner bear to no end.

"Do you have anywhere to stay?" Aidan asked finally, after watching her inspect her new workplace for a few painful seconds. He had no idea what expectations she might have had of the place, but was pretty sure the reality would have been a disappointment either way.

She turned and shook her head. Her expression didn't give him much to go on, except she didn't look all that pleased to be here.

"No problem. There are rooms upstairs. The stairs are through there." He gestured at the door near what was now her desk.

As usual, Jamie had been economical with the details about Aidan's new partner. Would it have killed him to mention that she was going to live here as well? He might have made sure the place looked a bit more presentable. No, actually that was a lie. Aidan would have done nothing of the sort, he would have left things as messy and dirty as they were now, because up until the point of actually meeting Heidi, he would have loved nothing more than to see her run right back out of the office, never to return.

"Thanks," Heidi repeated herself.

"Say, I was just going to head out for the night, how about we grab a bite to eat? I know this great pub nearby. Best fish and chips in town. My treat," Aidan suggested.

It immediately occurred to him that his offer might seem way too eager, but it was too late to worry about that now, since he'd already blurted it out.

"Through here?" Heidi asked, while turning the knob on the door leading to the stairs, as though she never even heard his invitation. She didn't wait for an answer either, and reached over to pick up her bag again before marching off into the dimly lit stairwell.

"Yeah, just take any room, they're all empty," Aidan called after her, just before the door shut behind her.

Very smooth, you idiot, he thought to himself while shaking his head. He could already tell that an uphill battle lay ahead if he was going to get along well enough with Heidi. She might be his mate, but she certainly wasn't all that friendly about it.

CHAPTER THREE

Heidi didn't know what to do. Should she take up Aidan on his offer of dinner? It would be the civil thing to do, and yet she really wasn't sure she was up to spending her evening socializing. All she really wanted was to crawl into the steel framed bed in the sparsely furnished room she found herself in, and hide under the covers.

So this was where she was going to stay and work...

It wasn't anything like what she thought a home ought to look like. Clearly this place could benefit from a feminine touch.

And Aidan? He seemed unusual, very unlike the boys she grew up with in Rannoch. Oddly enticing, like he was carrying a deep, dark secret that was just begging to be uncovered.

No way, that's just the hormones talking.

Heidi still couldn't believe that the first guy she ran into on her first stint in the outside world was going to be her mate. Fate was clearly playing a very cruel joke on her. She wanted to punch something - someone - and yet... She had to admit that he was rather handsome.

After lifting her bag onto the bed, she started unpacking the few belongings she had chosen to carry. All of it fit easily into the very impersonal steel filing cabinet in the corner - the only thing that could even be interpreted as storage in this room.

She hid her assortment of weapons underneath her clothes, and slammed the drawer shut with a loud crash that echoed off the bare walls.

There wasn't a sign of anything remotely nice in sight.

The bed was made of tubular steel with the occasional patch of rust breaking through the lacquer. The filing cabinet would have been primer gray at one point, except the paint had started to flake off, revealing the bare metal underneath. The room had no carpeting, dirty walls that probably hadn't seen a fresh coat of paint in years, and a bare bulb where a lampshade should have been.

The flooring provided the only source of color: a sea-green type of slippery vinyl that reminded her of the old school in Rannoch.

What a dump.

And the downstairs wasn't any better either. Worn desks with computers that looked at least ten years old, and all of it dusty. Didn't anyone ever clean this place? And was it just Aidan and Jamie working for the Alliance in Edinburgh, anyway? Quite a depressing presence for such an important city.

Heidi rubbed her eyes, which had gotten a bit sore after the long trip, and tried to focus on her last exchange with her dad before leaving.

Do your job, follow orders, do us proud, that's what he had said. *In the end, it's always us against them.*

It made perfect sense when she was still home, and she had been reasonably confident she would do a decent job. Now, she wasn't so certain anymore. How was she going to focus on her job, when a coworker provided such a big distraction?

Heidi took the mobile phone out of her pocket and stared at it for a while, before finally dialing home.

"Hello?" Heidi's mom answered almost immediately. She must have been sitting by the phone, waiting for this call.

"Hi, Mom," Heidi responded.

"You made it? Did everything go okay? How was the

trip?" So many questions, and Heidi didn't feel like answering them in much detail at all.

"Fine. I'm fine. I just wanted to let you know I'm here, before going out to dinner with the Alliance people."

"Oh, sure, darling. Well, take care of yourself, you're in the big city now."

After the emotional goodbye earlier today, this long distance exchange with her mother was difficult for Heidi. She struggled to keep it together, to answer concisely without letting the concern in her mom's voice tug at her emotions.

Between her confusing feelings for Aidan downstairs, the depressing room, and the uncertainty of whatever lay ahead, Heidi felt completely alone. This wasn't the beginning of an adventure as much as it felt like a banishment away from everything she knew.

"I will, Mom. I'll be fine," Heidi said, hanging up before one solitary tear escaped from the corner of her eye and rolled down her cheek.

This was hopeless. The longer she sat here on her own, the sorrier she would feel for herself and she did feel quite hungry... She dusted herself off, wiped her face with the back of her hand, and headed back downstairs. She could only hope Aidan hadn't left yet.

———◆———

"So, this is the place," Aidan said triumphantly, pointing at the gilded sign outside the historic looking building. Its name, The Coach and Horses, was written across an old fashioned illustration of the same.

Supposedly the best fish and chips in the city, though perhaps Aidan had just said that in an attempt to impress her, Heidi thought.

"Great," she responded, but her tone didn't quite match his excitement. She wasn't comfortable with the idea of sitting through dinner with the man, not because she didn't trust him, but because she couldn't trust herself.

"So where is - what do I call him? Mr. Abbott?" she asked, as they stepped through the wooden paneled door and into the cozy interior of the pub. It wasn't very busy inside, but Aidan opted to lead the way towards the back of the pub where there were even fewer people.

"Jamie. He... well, he keeps his own schedule. I should probably let him know you've arrived, though," Aidan said, while pulling out a chair for her at the nearest unoccupied table that caught his fancy.

"Sure." Heidi observed Aidan as he took out his phone and tapped out a quick message.

His movements, even while they were just walking the short distance between the office and the pub, seemed deliberate. Like he never did anything without a purpose. He gave the impression of a born predator with an iron focus. That's probably what struck Heidi the most about him, when she allowed herself to really watch the man. The wolves she grew up with, even those a generation before Heidi, were a lot more playful than Aidan seemed.

But his body language changed significantly when he was talking to her, like he wasn't being himself. They hadn't spoken about it yet, but she assumed that the strange pull she felt towards him was throwing him off balance as much as it did her. He was just a lot better at concealing that fact.

"Hi."

Heidi looked up to find a cheerful looking girl in a too tight white t-shirt and black apron featuring the pub's logo smiling down at her. "Ready to order?"

"Oh. Hi, Aidan, I didn't see you there," the girl added.

She blushed and looked away at her notepad, while scratching the side of her face with the back of her pen.

"I'll have the usual, please," Aidan said, while putting his phone away again. His eyes glanced up at the waitress, but then almost instantly settled on Heidi.

"You said the fish and chips were good here, right? So I guess that's what I'll have. And a Coke, please," Heidi said. Coke was the first thing that popped into her head. A big change from the largely homemade offerings of Rannoch, plus Heidi didn't drink, never had.

"Two fish platters, a Guinness and a Coke, coming right up." As soon as she finished repeating the order, the girl made a quick escape, and they were on their own again.

All the tables around them were empty, and despite the ambient noise of conversations, and cheers for some football game on the TV nearer the entrance, they might as well have been completely alone.

"What brings you here, anyway?" Aidan made a first attempt at small talk.

"What is a girl like me doing in a place like this, you mean?" Heidi teased, and immediately regretted it. This wasn't how you handled a professional dinner with a new coworker, not at all. *Stupid.*

"Something like that."

"I guess I want to make a difference," she said.

"Me too."

They stared at each other for just a moment too long, until Heidi caught herself and looked away. This really wasn't how she had imagined her first night in Edinburgh would go. She felt an urgent need to express how weird everything felt. So far away from everything she had known all her life.

She wondered if Aidan felt a similar conflict of

emotions towards her.

Did he even feel their connection like she did? All the stories she'd heard growing up told of these bonds being mutual. Always.

On the other hand, the way the waitress had acted around them just now suggested that perhaps he was just a little bit of a player. Perhaps he couldn't feel it. She'd be damned if she was going to be the first to say something if that were the case.

"Fancy finding you here," a male voice interrupted her thoughts.

Heidi looked up to find another huge man towering over their table. He was almost as broad and equally athletic as Aidan. The two were roughly the same height.

"Jamie." Aidan's voice sounded cheerful enough, but Heidi could detect a hint of displeasure in him anyway. "Meet Heidi. Heidi, this is Jamie Abbott."

"Oh, right," Heidi mumbled, while getting up and offering her hand to her new boss. Their boss.

She felt her cheeks burn up a bit, as though she had been caught. In this light, neither of them would be able to see that, right?

Jamie took her hand, shaking it firmly. "Welcome to the team, Heidi. Sorry I couldn't be there earlier when you arrived. I had some things to attend to."

"No problem. Nice to meet you."

Jamie pulled up a chair and joined them. "Organizing a welcome dinner without inviting me, huh? I'm surprised, Aidan."

"I couldn't let her go to bed hungry on her first day, could I? Just trying to be civil," Aidan protested.

Their banter would have seemed light-hearted to the casual observer, but Heidi found herself having a little extra insight, at least into Aidan's feelings about the matter.

He wasn't pleased at all that Jamie had turned up.

On the one hand, neither was Heidi, but on the other, she did feel a bit relieved. With him around, at least she'd be forced not to do anything stupid on her first night away from home.

Jamie ordered his dinner as well, along with a beer of some description, the name of which Heidi didn't recognize. The three of them chatted until the food arrived.

Apparently it wasn't just the two - now three - of them that were stationed in Edinburgh on Alliance business. There was another guy, their computer expert, Kyle, who was away visiting family. Heidi was the first female on the team. Quite the responsibility, she thought.

Throughout dinner, Heidi felt occasional glances and intermittent stares originating from Aidan's direction. Whenever Jamie asked her something, and Aidan was just observing, he kept observing her. It was unnerving, especially since she felt her body react involuntarily.

A persistent heat collected inside her lower abdomen, making her skittish and uneasy. She already knew Aidan could tell - that explained the dark stares - but could Jamie as well? Surely he'd be able to smell the change in her, if he paid just a little attention?

It was embarrassing to say the least but she couldn't control it. By the time dinner was done, and it was time for her to retreat to her room, she was relieved to get away from Aidan at least for the night.

How long until she could no longer control her urges? How long before *he* decided it was time to take action, even if she didn't?

CHAPTER FOUR

—— ◆ ——

After Aidan and Jamie had walked Heidi back to the office, leaving her there by herself with much difficulty, Aidan was much too restless to head home and go to bed himself. He said his goodbyes to Jamie, and instead he opted for a walk towards the center of town. The Alliance premises, which occupied one of the many downtrodden buildings near the harbor, was only a fifteen minute walk away from the city center.

The Alliance was on a budget, but that was only part of the reason why their office was in one of the less scenic areas of what was otherwise a very attractive city. Edinburgh attracted many tourists every year, and the Alliance was hell-bent on keeping a low profile. Luckily, these same tourists rarely ventured beyond the Castle, the Royal Mile and select other sightseeing hot spots in the area.

The diverse crowd made Edinburgh a nice place to stay for people - or bears - who enjoyed the company of others, but didn't like them to stick around long enough to ask awkward questions.

Aidan wandered the familiar streets heading towards the Old Town, passing by busy pubs and restaurants, many of which he'd visited previously. But he wasn't looking to join the bustling nightlife. He was after solitude - a chance to clear his head and think about all that had happened today. And of course, about Heidi.

Rather than turn onto the Royal Mile that led to Edinburgh Castle, he crossed the street and continued straight on towards Holyrood Park, a huge green patch right in the middle of the city that also contained Arthur's Seat, the distinctively shaped hill that could be seen from pretty much anywhere in Edinburgh.

Although it was a popular destination for tourists as well as anyone else looking for a bit of privacy like he was, it did get very quiet at night. It was the one place where Aidan occasionally allowed himself to shift, but only on dark, starless nights.

Tonight was one of those nights. He could hardly control the urge to let his bear out, and as luck would have it, the moon as well as stars were hidden behind a thick cloud cover typical for this time of year. Scotland was pretty well known for its wet and unpredictable weather, especially when the last of the late summer warmth had left the land.

By now, early October, there was very little chance of the weather clearing up, so Aidan felt safe to be himself, if only for a little while. The Code of Secrecy all shifters adhered to was important to Aidan, that's why he only did this very rarely. Too much had happened in recent years to be lax about shifting in full view. Even just a single human witnessing a transformation was one human too many.

When he reached the edge of the park, his brisk walk turned into an impatient jog. After ensuring he was completely alone, he hid behind some shrubs and got undressed, concealing his clothes in the fallen leaves. Then he closed his eyes and breathed a sigh of relief as his instincts took over.

Fur sprouted where there previously had been none. As did claws and teeth, strong and sharp enough to tear flesh and crunch bone. His body grew to almost twice its original size and when he opened his eyes again, the world around him seemed to have changed along with him.

Things made more sense now.

Aidan had never expected that he'd come face-to-face with fate today. If he was completely honest, he had never really believed that there was one true mate for every bear out there. It was a strange and wondrous thing, the feeling of knowing beyond a shadow of a doubt that someone was meant to be yours.

Heidi.

She'd tried her best to hide it, to pretend like everything was all right and she didn't feel the way he did, but she couldn't hide her physical reactions to his presence. She couldn't control her hormones, the slight blush of embarrassment when they were interrupted at the pub, the flutter in her heartbeat when she'd caught him staring at her from across the table.

If only Jamie hadn't shown up when he did, perhaps Aidan wouldn't have been alone tonight. After wandering much of Scotland, and parts of Europe on his own as though he didn't need anyone else in his life, he felt a strange urge to share this place with her.

She wasn't ready for it though, he knew that. He would give her some space to come to him. Fate had decided that they be together, but that didn't mean they had no choice in the matter at all. She had to come to the conclusion herself that this was what she wanted.

He deeply breathed in the fresh air in an attempt to calm himself. The scents of grass and heather, along with a bit of salt from the sea hung in the air. He enjoyed the feel of the soft muddy ground under his paws, he even allowed himself to scratch at one of the bigger trees in the area - something he didn't do normally for fear of humans discovering the marks.

Throughout his little expedition back to nature, Aidan kept his ears open for any sign of human activity. He was good at hiding in the darkness, but he was never careless.

Carelessness got you killed, he knew that.

Just as he was ready to leave again, his sensitive hearing picked up another presence further up the hill. Someone out for a late night walk up Arthur's Seat, perhaps? Two pairs of footsteps and muffled voices traveled down to his position. A couple, out for a quiet stroll?

Aidan stayed extremely still, and crouched down behind some of the shrubs set alongside one of the walking paths circling the hill. Sure enough, after a ten or fifteen minute wait, two men appeared in the distance. They were carrying flashlights to help them walk the difficult terrain, but Aidan would have seen them even without.

He ducked down behind the foliage, and just listened.

"Brother, I don't know if this is wise. It's been a while since we've had any action."

"That's exactly why it's time. Plus, those animals aren't going to wait for us to be ready. We should mobilize the old guard, as well as recruit a few new soldiers."

What the-? Aidan's heart started to beat faster. The way they spoke was eerily similar to some of the chatter on the message board he'd signed up on earlier. Could he accidentally have stumbled across a couple of members of the Sons of Domnall, just as they were planning to ramp up their activities?

"What about weapons?" asked one of the men.

"Leave those to me."

"All right. I'll start recruiting then."

"Good man. I'll be in touch when the leadership has formulated a plan."

Aidan took care not to disturb the shrubbery around him but couldn't resist a peek at the two figures ahead. Both of the men were white, one in his thirties, the other perhaps two decades older. They wore football shirts,

Aidan could just about make out the logo of one of the main clubs in the city.

They gave each other a quick hug and pat on the back, and the younger one walked on up the path. The older man turned to go back to from where they had just emerged, giving Aidan the chance to get a better look at his face just for a moment.

Something about him was familiar, but he didn't think he'd ever met the man. Aidan was good with faces, so to come across someone he thought he might have seen before, without being able to identify when or where, was unusual.

Who was that? And why did he look so familiar?

Aidan waited as both of the men vanished from view and even their footsteps faded away in the distance.

The conversation he'd overheard was vague and didn't even fully prove that they were who he suspected. Still, Aidan knew in his gut that this was the real deal. This was significant. He ought to report what he'd seen to Jamie.

After staying out of sight behind the bushes for another ten minutes, just in case, Aidan hurried back to where he'd left his clothes. He transformed back into his human form just as a slight drizzle started to fall.

It was during times like these he regretted having to act human for most of his life. As a bear, he wouldn't have cared at all about the rain, but there was hardly anything worse than trying to wear clothes on top of damp, shivering skin.

As soon as Aidan was dressed, he wrapped his coat around himself tighter to ward off the cold, and rushed back through the streets he'd walked earlier. Not home, but straight to the office.

———◆———

A few strong cups of coffee later, Aidan had opened the familiar news articles concerning his parents' deaths again. His recognizing the older one of the two men in Holyrood Park had something to do with the accident, he could feel it, but he couldn't pinpoint just why that might be.

Despite going over everything again and again, hoping for some kind of connection to form in his mind, he'd made no progress. Aidan already knew these pages by heart, so looking at them any further seemed like an exercise in futility.

Instead, he sat quietly in his chair, his eyes closed, and tried to remember everything he knew about the case. There was something missing. Something that the computer couldn't tell him. And then he realized what it was: the local paper that used to be delivered to the house when he was growing up didn't show up on any of the websites he'd found! He didn't even know for sure if it still existed.

Just after the accident, Aidan had collected every mention of his parents in the Isle of Skye Gazette. Every article and their obituary. The short feature on McMillan Farm that had served as a sort of memorial for his parents who, although private, had been well liked by the local community. He had to obtain those clippings to see if they could shed light on the matter.

Aidan checked his watch; 4 AM. It would be hours before either of his two colleagues would turn up to start their day. As soon as it was a halfway decent time, he would phone Jamie to let him know he needed to take a few days off. That would be the only way to put his racing mind at rest.

He crossed his arms and leaned back in the rickety office chair, in an attempt to catch some shut-eye. He couldn't find any peace though. In between images of the two men he'd seen at the park, glimpses of when he first saw Heidi mere hours ago infiltrated his frazzled mind.

Aidan hadn't wanted a partner, and especially not one new to the business. But knowing that she was safe upstairs made him feel more at home in this dingy office than he did whenever he visited the farm where he grew up. That was the thing about losing one's parents before their time: it could sour the idea of family… of home.

If he could just figure out just how their deaths fit into the grand scheme of things, perhaps he could move on and have a family of his own again. Perhaps that's why fate had sent Heidi his way now. Perhaps it hadn't been a coincidence, but perfect timing instead.

CHAPTER FIVE

It had been a long, largely sleepless night, followed by a painfully early morning. Heidi had stared aimlessly into the darkness of her room, until she must have dozed off for a while without realizing. The vivid images of Aidan, shirtless, hovering above her with a hungry look in his eyes had felt so real. When he leaned down to kiss her, it was as if she could taste his essence on her lips, feel the tickle of his breath against her skin.

Like he had actually been there with her all night.

Although even in the midst of these most intimate of dreams she was still painfully aware of how inappropriate their affair was, she hadn't been able to resist him. He had made her feel something she had never known: a sense of belonging and purpose that had nothing to do with her duty to her pack, but that answered a deeper need within herself. For just a little while, she had stopped feeling so alone in the world.

Morning came in the form of a panicked awakening sparked by… Well, Heidi wasn't sure by what, exactly. The building was quiet, it was still dark outside, and everything indicated that she was on her own.

All she knew for sure was that she had a throbbing headache, and felt uneasy about what the day had in store for her. But she couldn't bear lying in bed anymore either, so she got herself up, tried to stretch the lethargy out of her tired limbs and reluctantly climbed down the stairs.

Coffee, that would solve everything! Heidi could only hope that she would be able to find everything on her own, until one of the others came into the office.

"Oh!" Heidi exclaimed as soon as she stepped into the office, finding Aidan already sitting there poring over various printouts and websites on his computer screen.

He quickly closed whatever he had open on the PC, and rotated his chair to face her. "Morning."

He was wearing exactly the same clothes as yesterday. *Weird. Had he been here all night?*

"You're up early..." she remarked.

He just smiled, bleakly. Yeah, she was sure of it now, he had never left. If he hadn't looked so focused on his work just now, she might have wondered if coming back into the office was just an excuse to be in the same building with her. He seemed to have other things on his mind, though.

"Is something wrong?" she asked at last.

"Wrong? Not at all. Why don't you grab a seat and we can go over a few things." Aidan pointed at the wobbly looking chair sitting in front of what was going to be Heidi's desk and pulled out a few files and notes from the mess of paper in front of him. "Oh, if you want to grab a coffee, I've made some already."

Indeed the scent of freshly brewed coffee had already made it into Heidi's nose, so she quickly poured herself a cup and got her chair. As she sat down beside Aidan, something told her that this, the matter-of-fact workaholic investigator, wasn't a front, but really him. It was strange to admit it, but she liked it. Here was a guy who could take things seriously when required, unlike some of the boys she'd grown up around.

"Excuse me for jumping right into things, but we're in the middle of an investigation, as you will already know."

"The Sons of Domnall. Yes, I know," Heidi responded, trying her utmost not to get distracted by his presence so nearby. If she reached out just a little, she would accidentally brush against his arm... *Stop it!*

"Well, we've been trying to get close to them, at least on the Internet. We have an informant who has shared a couple of websites, and one of those hosts a message board that I have joined, pretending to be someone with - shall we say - similar interests and convictions." Aidan flipped open the first file, and showed her some print-outs from the websites in question.

"Okay." Heidi took the first sheet and studied the screenshots. The whole thing was quite vague, nowhere did it mention that these people knew about shifters, or were out to hunt them down. Of course they'd keep that kind of content locked away from the general public...

"They present themselves as ordinary right-wingers; racists and bigots," Aidan clarified, before she had the chance to voice her observations.

"I see."

He showed her another few sheets of paper which contained conversations - presumably printed from the message board, as well as a glossary containing phrases and words the members had used regularly.

"Has anyone made contact with you?" Heidi asked.

Aidan looked up, meeting her gaze with his. Their eye contact was almost painful, making her heart race and stomach flutter. Heidi quickly looked away again and reached over to pick up her coffee from the desk, knocking the cup over in the process and spilling the remainder of its contents across the floor.

"Oh, crap, I'm so sorry!" Heidi jumped up instantly, picked up the cup and set it aside, before looking around for a towel, or a cloth of any kind.

Aidan just observed her for a moment, before reaching into one of the drawers of his desk, taking out a large pack of paper napkins.

"Here you go," he said, his voice a lot gentler than it had just been when he was briefing her. How had he managed to switch from complete pro to warm and friendly in a split second?

His finger brushed past hers ever so gently when he handed her the napkins, sending shivers down her spine. She flinched and retreated instantly, but somehow something had changed in her. She felt like he was still touching her, even though they were at least three feet apart from one another.

No way, that was stupid. She was just tired, and the lack of sleep was starting to mess with her mind.

While she tried her best to contain the mess on the floor, he seemed to go right back into work-mode as if nothing had happened.

"One of the regular members of the message board has sent me a couple of messages, yes. Nothing beyond that, but I'm hopeful." Aidan took a deep breath, before continuing. "But that's not why I came in last night."

"No?" Heidi asked, while picking up the coffee-soaked napkins and putting them into the trash.

"I overheard a conversation, while I was out for a walk after dropping you here. The details are inconclusive, much like these websites are, but my instincts tell me there's something more to it. I may have accidentally stumbled across two of their members..."

Heidi stopped what she was doing and stared at him. *Wow, could it be?* Obviously this was what she was here for, to make a real difference, but she hadn't heard of the Alliance actually making much progress yet. To find that Aidan had come across some potential real life members of the Sons of Domnall on her first night in the city was incredible. She couldn't wait to tell her dad the good news.

"That's amazing! Does Jamie know? What are we going

to do, follow them?" Heidi asked.

Aidan shook his head throughout her questions and raised his hand, making a calming gesture. "There's no point in doing anything until my suspicions are confirmed. But there is something else..."

"What's that?" Heidi thought she could pick up on a vibe that told her he was about to share something significant.

"I think I may have recognized one of them," Aidan's voice was low, clearly this information was something he had intended to keep secret.

She didn't respond straightaway, and before she had the chance, the lock on the front door clicked, revealing a wind-blown Jamie Abbott.

"Morning, guys! You're up early!" Jamie greeted them with a wide grin, which to Heidi looked a bit off.

"That's what she said," Aidan remarked dryly while getting up from his chair.

Heidi nodded and smiled back at Jamie, while trying to figure out if she was just tired and hence seeing things that weren't actually there. He was nice enough, had been last night as well, but something made her feel like he was hiding something from the two of them. Perhaps she was just picking up on Aidan's emotions, who clearly preferred being alone with Heidi over having Jamie around.

It's all in your head, woman!

"I'd like a word, please," Aidan told Jamie, who nodded and followed Aidan into the stairwell, leaving Heidi on her own.

While the two were outside, Heidi wondered why she wasn't more curious about their exact conversation. Her instincts told her that Aidan had taken Jamie aside not to hide something from her, but to handle him. Why she would think that, she wasn't quite sure. It must have been a fated mate thing, some failsafe that ensured mates trusted each other implicitly.

Instead of pondering their strange relationship further, Heidi picked up some of the papers Aidan had showed her and started to read. She went through the glossary, the transcripts of various conversations between suspected Sons of Domnall members that had taken place on that message board, and finally, she studied the beginnings of a members list Aidan had put together.

They all used aliases, which didn't mean much to Heidi. Nobody had put up their own picture either, but Aidan had somehow managed to put together a few relevant details about each one of the people he'd followed online. Their profiles contained suspected locations, as well as age ranges for some of them based on turns of phrase or slang they used. Aidan had also added certain special skills to some of the profiles. If this information was true, it was impressive work. She did wonder if half of the details were just wild guesses, though.

By the time Aidan and Jamie appeared again, Heidi had already switched on her computer and started browsing the website and message boards herself.

"Heidi?" Jamie called out to her.

"Yes?" She got up and joined the two men in front of Aidan's desk.

"Aidan has just briefed me about an important development in our investigation. Unfortunately he has a family emergency to attend to, so he's going to be away for a few days. In the meantime you and I will work together."

Heidi looked up at Aidan, then back at Jamie. *A family emergency?* It didn't feel right, but from the look in Aidan's eyes she knew not to question Jamie's explanation. She would find out what was really going on when the time was right.

Jamie led her back to her desk and took a seat beside her, while Aidan busied himself stuffing various items into a worn leather shoulder bag.

She turned around, observing him for a moment. *Be safe,* she thought. Aidan looked up and shot her a subtle smile just when their eyes met. As though he had heard her. That couldn't be, though... could it?

"Let's go through the rest of these files together," Jamie said.

She turned back again and responded with a quick nod. "Okay."

Jamie opened another folder and handed it to her. Inside were pictures and names of people - shifters - who had gone missing under mysterious circumstances. She didn't recognize any of them, but felt deeply sad seeing their faces anyway. The list read "Suspected Sons of Domnall Victims" across the top.

Behind the two of them, the door creaked open, and then fell shut with a click, and Heidi felt that Aidan had gone.

CHAPTER SIX

The drive from Edinburgh to Aidan's home on the Isle of Skye was a long one. Six hours in the best of conditions, without taking any breaks. But these weren't the best of conditions...

By the time Aidan made it to the island, a storm was lashing the rugged landscape, making conditions treacherous at best, lethal at worst. He knew his brother Derek would have taken precautions, so he wasn't worried about what he'd find there. Still, it didn't help that the thick clouds overhead had made dusk arrive much earlier than normal.

The stores were always fully stocked with food, as well as firewood and other supplies they would need to weather a storm. Especially at this time of year, shortly before winter would properly set in, the farm would have everything he'd need. Although he didn't visit home nearly often enough, he could always count on a warm enough welcome, including good food, courtesy of his brother.

The landscape on the island was starkly beautiful: barren hills, covered with a smattering of heather and tough grasses, broken up only by the occasional patch of woodland. The black cliffs that rose up from the center of the island stood proudly against the dark gray skies, like timeless giants, bearing silent witness to whatever went on around them.

He kept on driving, despite the winds trying to push his car off the narrow road and into the nearest ditch, until finally Aidan had to admit defeat. With the woods surrounding McMillan Farm already in view, he parked his car to make the rest of the journey on foot. The trees were old, weathered - a legacy from Aidan and Derek's ancestors who had planted the first of them two centuries ago when they first settled here, and downed branches would make driving conditions even more treacherous up ahead.

The storm had brought in cooler air from the north, and rain and sleet would seep into Aidan's clothes, chilling him to his core. He knew what he had to do: if he wanted to make it home safely, he had to shift.

Still in the car, safe from the elements, Aidan got undressed. A deep breath later, he stepped out into the icy cold, and let his instincts do the rest.

The entire process was over in less than a second; the cold was a brilliant motivator for quick shifts. He started to run in the direction of the farm, his paws carrying him over the mossy, wet ground much faster than human feet could have. Plus, he didn't have to worry about the cold creeping into his muscles, slowing him down.

Although the roads would be empty in these conditions, he kept off them anyway out of habit, which was just as well because his car wasn't the only one out this evening. A gray hatchback stood still in the middle of the road just inside the woods, its lights still on and filtering through the rain.

Aidan's heart started to race. He checked the car from afar first, then investigated it up close once he realized there was no sign of life anywhere around it. He could smell blood. Human. But whoever had been in the car at the time of the accident wasn't around anymore.

He decided to get back on course to his original destination, home. Aidan couldn't explain it, but he felt that something had gone very wrong.

Still anxious, Aidan entered the farmhouse in a rush. Coming up the drive, he had seen that most of the house was dark, save for a dim light in the bedroom and the kitchen. The storm must have knocked out the power. When he found the kitchen empty, save for a pot bubbling away on the fire, he proceeded down the hall and burst into Derek's room. Nothing could have prepared Aidan for what awaited him.

In the bed sat a woman, her mouth wide open in shock. The bright red bruise on her forehead stood out against her pale skin. Aidan stared at her, equally surprised, then spied his brother's form lurking in the corner of the room, as if he'd been guarding the female.

"Aidan. Bad timing," Derek growled.

"Well... This is awkward," Aidan responded.

They weren't very close, Aidan and his brother, but Aidan just couldn't imagine Derek and this woman... Derek had never shown interest in the opposite sex. While Aidan had been the more curious one, Derek had been content tending the farm on his own. *So, what was different about her?*

"A word, please?" Derek said. Aidan agreed and they both exited.

"She's human," Aidan said as they made it into the hallway, shutting the bedroom door behind them, and immediately shifted into his human form again.

"I know."

"She's seen us." The more Aidan thought about it, the more he realized the disaster he had gotten himself into. It was obvious that the car wreck on the road had belonged to this woman; she had the cut on her head to prove it.

And yet he had marched into the house as a bear, expecting that Derek was on his own like he always was. *Stupid.*

They moved into Aidan's old room and got dressed. As Aidan continued to question his brother, and Derek kept insisting that she was a guest who had rented one of the cottages, he was certain that there was something else Derek wasn't telling him. So what if she was a tourist? So what if she crashed her car? None of that explained why she was in Derek's bed rather than her own.

It was then that Derek turned the tables on Aidan and started asking *him* questions. *Why are you here?* There was something in Derek's tone that made Aidan defensive. As if he had to have a reason to come home.

Still, being vague about everything wasn't going to help any. As Aidan and Derek finally headed into the cozy kitchen for some much needed warmth and nourishment, Aidan felt it was time to share at least some of his recent activities with his brother.

He was going to tell him about his job at the Alliance, but it was Derek who spoke first.

"She's my mate, Aidan." Derek's words explained everything.

He started to clarify how he felt, but Aidan didn't need further details to know exactly what was going on. The way Heidi had made Aidan feel from their very first meeting onward had driven him to act out of character too. Now that the woman, whose name turned out to be Clarice, had seen the two of them as bears, there was no turning back either. Derek wouldn't let her go, that much was obvious. He couldn't, just as Aidan couldn't ignore his feelings for Heidi.

When it was Aidan's turn to speak, he indeed opened up to his brother. About the Alliance, and their work with the Sons of Domnall. Aidan didn't believe in fear-mongering, but it was only sensible to inform people, and especially Derek, so that he could prepare himself.

But Aidan's concerns about exposing his real self to a human didn't fade. Derek would never be able to do anything to harm Clarice, the woman, because she was his mate. But would the same rules apply to her? He tried to tell Derek about the dangers that existed nowadays. How the Sons of Domnall had actually been hunting shifters, so the Code of Secrecy all shifters lived by had become doubly important. You never knew who was watching, or whom to trust. As far as Aidan was concerned, any human was a potential threat.

"I'm not sure we can trust her," Aidan insisted.

"I am," Derek responded.

Something in Derek's eyes had changed, a glow that hadn't been there before. Bears' eyes glowed when they were in danger, angry, or otherwise riled up. But Derek's body language wasn't threatening. When a female voice started to speak from behind Derek, all was explained.

Clarice, the human, had woken up and found her way into the kitchen. As she started to speak, Aidan could see that there was something more to them than what he'd witnessed of human relationships. They acted like mates, seemed to know the other's thoughts. She said their secret was safe with her, and sounded pretty damn convincing.

Aidan decided to give them the benefit of the doubt, for now. What was he to do, anyway? Tell the Alliance? Try to scare Clarice away in the hopes that she wouldn't return? In his work with the Alliance, Aidan had seen what happens to shifters who lose a mate. It wasn't pretty. There was no way he could do that to his own brother.

"I think I'm going to give you two some space," Aidan said, sensing that his presence was no longer wanted.

Neither of them responded, in fact they acted like he had never even been there.

Aidan walked down the hall straight to his old bedroom. He'd come here for a reason, and the unfortunate incident earlier had thrown him off track long enough. He didn't think either Derek or Clarice would come looking for him tonight, but he felt compelled to lock his door anyway.

Once safe, he switched on an emergency lantern on the bedside table. It wasn't bright, but it was enough for Aidan to start emptying the large wardrobe that contained all his old things.

On the top shelf, behind stacks of old woolen sweaters and other winter clothes, sat an old cookie tin. This is where he'd kept all of the newspaper clippings just after the accident. He hadn't looked at it in years, and opening that box was never easy for him.

He carried it over to the leather arm chair in the corner and held his breath as he flipped the lid open. Inside, everything was as he remembered. Newspaper articles, sorted by date of publication, and bundled according to which paper they'd come from. And a sealed envelope.

He weighed the envelope in his hand. It was heavy, which was only natural considering its content, and inspected the seal. The red wax was still intact, and looked exactly the same as the day when their cousin, Elise, had handed it to him for safekeeping. He set it aside and continued to rifle through the contents of the box.

Underneath all the papers, he found the gold locket his mother had always worn. The policeman who had come to the farm to notify them of what had happened had given that to him. Although not strictly relevant to his mission, he opened the pendant anyway. Inside, exactly as he remembered, was a photograph of his dad on the left and one of Derek and himself, when they were only boys, on the right.

It hurt. Seeing these things always hurt.

He quickly shut the pendant again and placed it back into the bottom of the tin, and started going through the various clippings instead. It didn't take him long to find exactly what he was looking for: one of the first articles in the Isle of Skye Gazette, titled *Tragic Road Accident Claims Two Lives*.

The article was accompanied by a photograph of the wreckage, along with a man in a firefighter uniform. Bingo.

Aidan squinted at the picture, but it remained as grainy as ever. He was certain that this was the same man he'd seen in Edinburgh the other night. Neither the caption, nor the article mentioned him by name.

This could not be a coincidence. After all these years, following instinct alone, he finally had some proof: their parents' death had been no accident.

CHAPTER SEVEN

Heidi's second morning at the Alliance office wasn't perfect, but at least she'd slept well enough. Somehow, knowing that Aidan was going to be gone for a couple of days had helped her relax.

She was up by seven and headed straight down to find the office eerily quiet. After figuring out how to work the coffee machine, she settled down into her chair and looked through the files she'd started working on yesterday. The news that Aidan might have found actual Sons of Domnall members running around Edinburgh had been very exciting indeed.

The one thing she didn't understand was why Aidan had run off all of a sudden, giving Jamie some nonsense excuse about a family emergency. She couldn't explain how she knew, but there was no family emergency. It had something to do with the job, she was convinced of it.

It was too bad they hadn't had the chance to talk further until Jamie came in, or she might have known more about what exactly Aidan had seen, and what he thought it meant. Still, just because Aidan wasn't here, didn't mean Heidi had to sit around doing nothing. She knew about the websites, she had read the files Aidan and Jamie had given her, and she was plenty motivated to get started and make some real progress.

She had only taken a few sips of her hot coffee by the time she logged on to the main website. *A profile.* She needed to create a profile for herself, just like Aidan had done. Heidi made a few notes, picking phrases from Aidan's glossary that she felt would make her sound authentic.

Although the member profiles of the other people on the website were vague at best, Heidi opted to fill out the "gender" field anyway. Perhaps they'd be more inclined to talk to a new *female* member? That was how the world worked, wasn't it?

Once her profile was set up and her introduction typed out, she sat back, lukewarm cup in hand and admired her handiwork. Not a bad start.

Rather than wait around for responses - she couldn't imagine any of these people would log on so early in the morning anyway - Heidi started working on something else that had been bothering her ever since she'd arrived day before yesterday: the state of the office.

She began with her new desk, but as soon as she'd gotten into the swing of things; tidying up papers, throwing away random bits of rubbish, and wiping the top down with a moist cloth, she found it hard to stop just there. She moved on to the coffee maker and stationary cupboard, then finally sorted out the final empty desk in the corner of the room, until everything looked clean.

Everything except Aidan's and Jamie's desks. She didn't dare touch those.

Just as Heidi poured herself a second cup of coffee, Jamie arrived.

"Morning," he said, as he started removing his coat, hanging it up on the shabby rack near the door.

"Morning," Heidi responded, observing the man as he walked across the office, straight to the coffee maker, pouring himself a large one. She counted six heaped teaspoons of sugar, and although she really wanted to comment on it, she kept quiet. *He's the boss. None of my business.*

After the first sip, followed by a satisfied sigh, Jamie

turned in Heidi's direction and caught her still staring at him.

"What?"

Heidi glanced away, embarrassed he'd busted her. "Nothing."

"Oh, the coffee? Did you want a refill?" Jamie asked, in between further sips of what must have been the sickliest sweet hot beverage Heidi had ever seen anyone drink.

"No, it's nothing, really." Heidi felt her cheeks burn up. *Crap.* She might as well explain herself, before he drew even worse conclusions. "Just, I've never seen anyone add that much sugar..."

Jamie let out a laugh and wandered over to his desk, placing the cup down and taking a seat in the much too small looking office chair, which groaned under his weight.

"That's the thing about bears, we have a giant sweet tooth," he remarked, while picking up his cup again and holding it in both hands.

Bears... Heidi's heart started to beat faster. That was right, Jamie was a bear; the first one she'd ever met. In all the confusion over the past few days, she never stopped to wonder about working in such close proximity with a bear, when for the most part, their species didn't get along very well. Perhaps that's why Aidan didn't trust Jamie fully either...

"No need to look so uncomfortable. We don't bite." Jamie winked at her, and leaned forward to switch on his computer. "In fact, Aidan and I fully stand behind the truce. We're better off working together, don't you think? As it is, the humans outnumber all of us."

The way he said it: *Aidan and him... As if... Holy Crap!*

If Heidi had managed to maintain at least some of her composure earlier, every last bit of it was gone now. She felt her chest tighten and her airways narrow. *That meant*

Aidan was a bear, too!

"Heidi? Are you all right?" Jamie asked.

Her vision blurred a bit, her head went fuzzy, and although she could hear his chair creak as he presumably got up, followed by footsteps in her direction, she couldn't bounce back and act normal.

"Fine. I'm fine!" she heard herself say, but it didn't sound convincing even to her own ears.

Of course Aidan was a bear. That's why he smelled different. That's why he was pretty much the same height and build as Jamie, taller as well as broader than most wolves. How the hell had she not noticed that before?

"Here, have some water." Jamie handed her a half-empty plastic bottle, which she accepted with trembling fingers.

"Thanks," Heidi mumbled.

Deep breaths, she told herself. *Deep breaths, calm down...* How could she calm down, though, when for some stupid reason she the man she was meant to mate with was a bloody bear?! Not just a colleague, but a bear on top of it! There had to be some way out of this mess. There was no way she would ever be able to show her face in Rannoch again if she paired up with a bear.

When the world came back into focus, she could see Jamie towering over her, with a concerned expression on his face.

"I'm okay, really," she said, while returning the water to him. "Low blood sugar. I haven't had breakfast."

"Ah, well that's understandable. How about we head out and rectify that, huh?" Jamie suggested.

Although it had been just an excuse, Heidi's stomach was indeed growling as well. She nodded, and got up to grab her things. She was still a little wobbly on her feet, but determined to follow along with her chosen cover story.

What Jamie had said was proven true after reaching the nearby cafe: bears evidently did have a massive sweet tooth. While Heidi opted for a full breakfast with extra sausages and bacon, Jamie ordered a huge stack of pancakes just for himself.

Bears...

———— ◆ ————

Later that afternoon, Heidi was still upset about the bear thing, obviously. But at least Aidan wasn't around to send her instincts into a tailspin. She'd been resisting him so far, how hard could it be to continue? Perhaps if she just worked hard enough, she could keep herself focused on the job alone.

Growing up, she'd heard a lot of stories about bears. They're lazy, greedy, anti-social... But now that she was working more closely with one, she had to wonder how much of that stuff was true.

Jamie seemed to be quite a reasonable person, save for his strange appetite and occasional grouchiness. He was easy enough to work with, and patient as well. So was Aidan, though. Kind, caring, and just reserved enough to be mysterious... And so very sexy. *Stop it! Stop getting distracted! You're not mating with a bloody bear!*

Heidi took a deep breath and tried to focus on her screen again. Luckily, her earlier prediction about females getting more attention online had proved to be true. Just eight hours after first signing up she had already received a bunch of responses from other members on the suspected Sons of Domnall message board. It was way more than Aidan's introductory post had received in days.

A lot of it was small talk, racist-style, but some people seemed eager to chat with her in more detail. She kept reading up on them, looking through Aidan's notes as well as existing discussions on the website, hoping to absorb as much of it as possible, while occasionally typing out hopefully authentic-sounding responses to everyone who had gotten in touch.

Time seemed to pass quickly, until finally later that same evening, the unthinkable happened: a private message arrived from one of the senior members of the forum.

A few of us are getting together tomorrow. Just drinks among friends, would you like to come along?

A sense of achievement welled up in Heidi's chest, or maybe nerves. Perhaps a bit of both. This was huge, exactly what they'd been working towards. Never once did she expect to get results this quickly, though.

"Hey, Jamie," Heidi called out, while waving at him excitedly.

Jamie looked up from his phone - who knows what he had been doing on there for the best part of the last hour. "What have you got?"

"I've got a way in with these people. They've invited me for drinks," Heidi explained.

Jamie got up from his chair and walked up behind Heidi, looking over her shoulder at the screen. He took a moment to read through the message, then Heidi showed him the discussion she'd been having publicly on the forum.

"Wow, great work." He patted Heidi on the back and pulled up a chair next to her. "Just a couple of things..."

"Yes?" Heidi asked.

"These are potentially dangerous people, but I don't have to tell you that, do I?"

"Indeed." Heidi nodded.

"And they're expecting you to go in alone, presumably."

"Presumably."

"How are your fighting skills?" Jamie asked.

Heidi shrugged. She'd been training for years, with various weapons as well as hand-to-hand. Everyone in Rannoch knew how to fight. "I'm pretty decent. Easily the strongest in my class."

Jamie smiled. "Your father did tell me that, but I wanted to hear it from you. Very well, then. Keep it simple: in and out, say a few hellos, try to remember as many faces and names as you can, then report back to me. Do not under any circumstance engage them, understand?"

"I understand." Heidi forced a smile. She understood the potential danger she could get into. If they were Sons of Domnall members, and they suspected any foul play at all, things could go very badly for her. She only hoped she was a good enough actress to convincingly disguise her true intentions. "No problem, I'll handle it."

"Good girl." Jamie got up and gave her a final nod. "I suggest you take it a little easy tomorrow, so you're well rested for the meeting in the evening."

CHAPTER EIGHT

Although the storm had calmed down overnight, Aidan hadn't been able to catch much sleep. Yesterday's discovery had been simply too exciting, and his mind kept racing to come up with a plan to identify the man in the picture. So, Aidan was already up and enjoying a hearty breakfast in the farm kitchen by the time anyone else stirred.

"Morning," Aidan greeted his brother, who had wandered in topless and half asleep.

"Mhm," Derek responded, while pouring two cups of coffee.

Behind him, a slightly disheveled looking Clarice came into the kitchen and eyed Aidan suspiciously. "Morning."

She was wearing a t-shirt big enough that it could pass as a nightie. One of Derek's, no doubt. Aidan nodded at her and started clearing up his used dishes, keeping them in the dishwasher. *Awkward* seemed too weak a word to describe the current atmosphere.

"I'm sorry if I seemed hostile last night," Aidan attempted to break the ice. "I was just concerned. This is all new to me."

"I understand," Clarice responded.

"No reason to be concerned," Derek added, while putting his arm around Clarice's shoulders. They did look happy together, like there was nothing else in the world that they could ask for. This was the kind of happiness you only saw between true mates.

Aidan shot them a bittersweet smile. His own mate was hundreds of miles away. A day's drive, but even when they were in the same room together, the distance between them seemed insurmountable. She had to come to him willingly, he reminded himself. He couldn't - wouldn't - force her.

"So, did you find whatever it was you were looking for last night?" Derek asked. He had a way of getting right to the heart of things.

Aidan glanced at Clarice, then reminded himself that they wouldn't have any secrets between them anyway, so he might as well tell both of them together.

"Yes. Have a look." Aidan sat down again and leaned over to retrieve the clear plastic folder with the newspaper clipping he'd found out from his shoulder bag, which was hanging from the back of the chair. Placing it down on the table, he slid it forward as Derek and Clarice both pulled up some chairs and sat down as well.

"This man." Aidan tapped on the picture with his index finger. "I saw him in Edinburgh two days ago. Overheard him discussing an attack."

"Wow." Derek picked up the folder and squinted at the picture, then passed it to Clarice. "You're absolutely sure?"

"I never forget a face."

"What does it all mean?" Clarice asked.

"Where do I begin? What does she know?" Aidan asked Derek.

"I overheard quite a bit last night, sorry about that." Clarice averted her eyes.

Derek took her hand and squeezed it encouragingly. "There shouldn't be any secrets between us. It's fine."

"So, I suspect that this man, and the one he was with in Edinburgh are members of the Sons of Domnall."

"Those are the people who hunt shifters, right?" Clarice asked.

Aidan nodded. "Yes. If he was around when our

parents were killed, it wouldn't be such a big stretch to think he might have had something to do with it. Maybe he found out who they really were somehow."

"Right..." Derek scratched his chin, like he often did when lost in thought. "One thing doesn't make sense to me. If he figured out Mom and Dad were bears, why not kill us too? Why let us live?"

"That, I don't know... If I find him, I'll make sure to ask him that." Aidan shook his head. That was strange indeed. He hadn't even considered that point. Trust his brother to find holes in his seemingly air-tight theory...

"So now that you've found this, what's next?" Clarice asked.

Aidan looked up at her. "I find out who he is. Get a name."

"Of course." Clarice sat back and held her coffee in both hands, staring at nothing in particular in the distance.

"Well, if I'm going to be successful, I'd better be off. Who knows what the storm has done to the roads." Aidan took the folder, put it back in his bag and got up. "I'll let you know what happens."

Derek got up as well, and the two brothers hugged each other goodbye.

"Clarice." Aidan nodded at her.

"Bye, Aidan," she responded.

Aidan picked up his bag, slung it over his shoulder and made his exit.

———◆———

The small town of Portree, about an hour's drive from the farm, might be the biggest settlement on the Isle of Skye, but it was still small by most people's standards. With a population of just under 2500 people, you could drive through the place in minutes.

Still, it was exactly here that Aidan expected to find his answers.

He drove up to the fire station, the only one on the entire island and hence the one that would have dealt with his parents' accident. If anyone knew who the man in the photograph was, it would be these people.

Everything looked quiet. There was no sign of any activity inside, and no cars parked in the marked bays next to the building. Aidan walked to the main entrance only to find it locked. Of course. Fire stations in small towns like this didn't have permanent staff, they just called people in whenever there was an emergency.

On the wall next to the bright red entrance door, there was a sign with a phone number to call if one needed assistance. Aidan took out his phone and dialed without hesitation.

"Hello?" a female voice answered after just a couple of rings.

"Hello there, I'm here at the fire station and I was wondering if I could talk to someone to help me identify one of your former firefighters?" Aidan responded.

There was a pause, and a low crackle in the line.

"To what end?" the woman asked.

To what end indeed. Aidan couldn't very well tell her the whole truth, so he opted for a partial version of it.

"Around fifteen years ago my parents were killed in a traffic accident on the island. I would like to speak to the man who was there. I have a photograph."

"I see..." she paused again. "Fine. I will be there in a little while."

The call was cut with a rustle and a click, and Aidan was left pacing the fire station parking lot back and forth on his own. He hoped she would be willing to help him out. And if she did, he hoped that the man in the photograph had actually been a real firefighter, not just someone dressed in a fake uniform.

But that wasn't his only concern: Derek was right. Why kill their parents and leave Derek and him alive? If the Sons of Domnall were trying to cleanse the world of all shifters, they should have come to the farm and finished the job just as soon as they found out that his parents had left two sons behind.

"Mister?" A voice called out to him from behind.

He turned to find a middle-aged woman standing a few feet away. She looked to be in her fifties, her long gray hair tied into a pony tail, and slightly dusty clothes that could only be described as 'sensible'.

"Forgive me, I was doing a bit of gardening when you phoned." She stretched out his hand towards him for a handshake.

"No problem. Aidan McMillan," he introduced himself.

"Helen Brown," she responded, while scrutinizing him over her small red-rimmed reading glasses. "Please tell me again what's the matter."

"You probably wouldn't remember, but fifteen years ago, my parents, Gillian and Matthew McMillan were killed in an accident on the A850..."

"I remember. Terrible business."

"It's been very difficult for my brother and me to come to terms with it, especially him since he was only a teenager when it happened. So, I was hoping to speak with the man who recovered the wreckage."

"I understand." She pushed her glasses further up the bridge of her nose and rummaged around in her handbag, retrieving a bunch of keys. "Why don't we discuss this inside?"

Aidan followed the woman as she unlocked the door,

and walked into the dark, empty fire station. Through the hallway, towards the left, she opened another door leading to an office, where she offered Aidan a seat.

"How about a cup of tea?" she gestured at the kettle in the corner.

Aidan nodded and sat down, while taking in his surroundings. There were photographs on the walls, group shots with little captions that were hard to read from where he was sitting.

"So who is this fellow you're trying to find then?" the woman asked, while dropping teabags into two empty mugs. "Sugar?"

"Yes please. Two. Well, as I said, I have this photograph. I apologize, it's not very clear..." Aidan took the folder with the newspaper cutting out of his bag and placed it on the desk ahead of him.

The woman leaned over to look at it, then turned back to face the kettle when it clicked to tell her the water had boiled. "I see. Don't think I know the man."

"If you could take a look again, I'd really appreciate it."

The woman turned around again, mugs in hand, and slid one of them towards Aidan. "You understand I can't just hand out contact information for former firefighters. It's against the rules."

Brilliant. The rules. "I just wanted to ask him a few questions. Thank him for his assistance in the matter. That's all."

She wrapped her fingers around her mug and cocked her head to the side. Then she looked up across the room, seemingly aimlessly as she spoke. "I want to help you, I really do, but I can't jeopardize my job here. It's a nice bit of extra change, you understand. Especially since my husband has had to stop working, it's been a great help to us."

"I understand. I don't want to cause any trouble for you." Aidan sighed.

"I think I need more milk in my tea, but I'm all out. Be a dear and wait here while I get some more..." The woman placed her mug down on the desk, while still staring across the room, then walked out, leaving Aidan on his own.

What had she been looking at so intently? Aidan scanned the wall behind him, then got up for a better look. There it was, another one of those group photos, this one labeled "Portree Fire Station, 1998". Among the dozen or so men portrayed, in the back row, third position from the left, there was a familiar face. Much clearer than the newspaper photograph, and unmistakably the same man that he'd seen in Edinburgh, only a bit younger of course.

The caption underneath gave Aidan everything he'd come here for. He counted the names written underneath. Back row, third from the left: Lee Campbell. He repeated it a few times in his head. *Lee Campbell, member of the Sons of Domnall, shifter killer.*

Aidan never forgot a face, and rarely forgot a name, especially one so important, but he felt the need to record this new find anyway. While listening out for footsteps signaling the woman's return, he quickly whipped his phone out of his pocket and took a picture of the entire group photograph, and another one of just the caption containing the names.

Who knows, perhaps this Lee Campbell person hadn't worked alone. Perhaps someone else in this picture had something to do with the accident?

Aidan quickly emptied his cup of tea, retrieved the folder with the newspaper clipping from the desk and stuffed it into his bag. He left without even catching a last glimpse of the woman who had helped him.

If he hurried, he could still make it to the town hall,

and hopefully get some more information about this Lee Campbell character, before starting his journey back to Edinburgh. If all went well, he would even be able to catch a good shut-eye before going back to work in the morning.

CHAPTER NINE

Everything had seemed okay, at least at first. Heidi kept going over it in her head but still couldn't understand exactly where things had gone as horribly wrong as they had. One moment, she was being introduced to people over drinks and small talk, the next, they were dragging her into a dark alley with a bag over her head and stuffing her into a van.

And now, who knows how many hours or days later - it was hard to keep track of time when locked up in a windowless room - Heidi still had no idea what these people wanted from her. Nobody had come in to talk to her, nobody had even given her anything to eat or drink. She was parched, starving, and close to giving up.

Despite how things turned out, she still was pretty sure she hadn't slipped up. Throughout the brief meeting at the pub, she'd stayed in character perfectly. So how did they know to suspect anything? Were they perhaps just being cautious?

The worst part was, the longer she was stuck here, the more her inner wolf fought to come out. If her captors only had a vague suspicion so far, a transformation would definitely push them into action. They would kill her, Heidi was certain of it. These were not people you messed with, especially if you were a shifter.

A loud click and creak interrupted her panicked thoughts, and the heavily reinforced door swung open. *Finally.*

"So, young lady, are you ready to tell us who you are yet?" The older guy she'd met at the pub walked in, flanked by two of the younger ones who had also been there earlier.

Heidi tried to focus her frazzled mind, so that she might remember every detail about these people. Although it was dark, her vision was much better than that of the humans, so she barely stirred, just observed from the bed she'd been shackled to.

Shaved heads, all of them, making it hard to figure out what their original hair color would have been. The younger guys had lots of tattoos, the sleeve type that covered their entire arms - at least as far as Heidi could see. The older one - she estimated him to be about fifty - also had a tattoo on his arm, but one of those old school, simpler ones. A couple of swallows holding a banner with the initials A. C.

"Not talking yet, I see. We have ways of making people change their minds," the older guy, presumably their leader, hissed.

"I don't know what you're talking about. I'm just concerned about where this country is headed, like you are. We can't stand by while we're overrun by those animals-" Heidi rambled.

"Quiet! There's something not right about you... You're not a copper, are ya?"

Heidi blinked a few times. They think she's police?

"Look, you invited me. If you thought I was up to no good, why do that?" Heidi pleaded.

"How did you find out about the message board?"

That was a good question indeed, one that she hadn't rehearsed an answer for... "A friend... a like-minded friend tipped me off to it. He said he'd come across it while browsing. He's a lot better with computers than I am, I don't know..." Her stomach growled, painfully. *Focus. Don't shift.*

"What friend?"

Heidi pressed her lips together tightly. She had nothing. If she mentioned any of the handles of other members of the message board, she had no way of knowing if this guy knew those people personally and would be able to verify that she was lying. There was only one name, one username that she knew for sure didn't belong to any of these people's associates... Aidan's.

"He goes by 'Fight4Independence', that's all I know," Heidi whispered. She felt bad that she had to ruin his cover too, but she had to give these people something, anything to go on that would sound plausible. This way, perhaps she'd get out of this yet, or at least buy some time to think up an escape plan.

The man didn't respond, just turned on his heel and left her cell again, followed by his two silent henchmen. A loud creak and click from the lock later, and Heidi was alone again.

Heidi breathed a sigh of relief. At least they had just questioned her and not done anything to hurt her. Perhaps they'd believe her story, and let her go. *That was still possible, right?* Or maybe they were planning to just let her rot here until she starved to death...

She flopped back onto the hard mattress and covered her eyes with the back of her hand to soothe the dull ache that had started to develop in her temples.

Ironically, the decor of her cell wasn't so different from her accommodation at the Alliance, with one exception: the mattress was even worse. She curled up on her side and tried to ignore the poking from the springs trying to break free from their flimsy covering.

If she could stick to her story, perhaps there was still hope, but with every passing moment, it became more and more difficult to stay positive. Unless she could get out of here soon, there was only one possible outcome. Sooner or later the wolf would win. And the man with the swallow tattoo would come in and put her down like a rabid dog.

Heidi thought back to what had led her here. Leaving Rannoch for the first time, saying goodbye to her family for who knows how long - potentially forever, considering her current situation. The Alliance office, and… Aidan.

Aidan, who had received her on that first night in Edinburgh, and made sure she got a good meal in her at a time when she felt more alone than she'd ever felt. She could almost taste that first meal all over again.

Aidan, who by all accounts seemed to be a complete professional, and capable member of the Alliance, but who hid a passion she'd never known before - the brooding looks he'd given her over that first dinner were as clear a sign as she needed.

And yet, he hadn't acted. He'd kept his distance, and treated her with respect. Was it because he was a bear and she was a wolf and he knew nothing good could come from it? No, if that had been the case, he wouldn't have been so kind to her.

She knew that if they gave in to their instincts and paired up, it would go against everything she'd been taught. It would even go against the rules put in place by the truce between their species.

Just because they were working together as part of the Alliance, didn't mean their species had all of a sudden forgot centuries of rivalries. If she followed fate and paired up with Aidan, she could never go home. She would never see her family again.

But as things stood now, and she was faced with the very real possibility that she'd never see any of them again, what hurt more? Realistically, the moment she left Rannoch, she'd changed forever. She would never be her parents' little girl again. She already didn't conform to what was expected of a she-wolf in Rannoch. She didn't want to play second fiddle to a man who would decide everything for her and their future children.

She wanted Aidan.

More than anything, it dawned on her that perhaps that was why fate had chosen him for her. They were mates, which meant that everything she had felt, he had felt too. He would have wanted to claim her from the moment he saw her, but he didn't. He had waited.

Tears started to burn in the corner of her eyes as she let her imagination take over. If they got together, he'd continue to respect her like that, she just knew it. He would treat her as an equal, not as a submissive. Perhaps that was why wolves didn't like bears and vice versa, their ways of life clashed too much. But Heidi wasn't an ordinary wolf...

In a last ditch attempt to keep her emotions in check, she tried to quit crying, but it was pointless. Tears were flowing more heavily now, running down the side of her face and into the dirty mattress. Perhaps this was for the best. If she vented like this, perhaps she could stay in control of her animal side a little bit longer.

Heidi lay there, curled up and motionless except for the occasional sob, until her body and mind tired and pulled her into a confused dream-state. Visions of Aidan filled her thoughts.

He opened the door to her cell, came inside and scooped her up in his strong arms. As he lifted her, the world spun out of focus and what had been just dirty bare concrete turned into a lush, green forest. Like the one in Rannoch. She looked up at his face, and saw that he was smiling down at her.

"I'm so glad I found you," he said.

She smiled back at him, closed her eyes and wrapped her arms around his shoulders. Those strong, muscular shoulders she'd previously only stolen glimpses at, but never touched. She'd been missing out.

Her head rested against his chest, which might as well have been made of steel. Rock hard muscles, all over. What a specimen. Gorgeous. All hers.

"I'm getting you out of here, don't worry," Aidan whispered in her ear, before stealing a kiss on that most sensitive of spots just down the side of her neck.

It tickled, and she couldn't suppress a giggle. "I know. I'm waiting for you."

That heat she'd first felt when she sat across from Aidan on her first night in Edinburgh in that pub had made a return. An intense fire burned in her, lighting up her lower abdomen. There was just one way to soothe it. One man who could soothe it.

She opened her eyes again and found Aidan staring down at her. His normally brown eyes had turned a deep, dark black. Just looking into them gave Heidi shivers.

The air seemed to prickle with tension, like the kind you feel in the calm before the storm.

His scent overwhelmed her senses. Sweet with a bit of spice. A little woody, like a forest in the fall after shedding all its leaves.

She chuckled.

"What?" he asked.

"You bears, you even smell *sweet." Heidi grinned up at him.*

Aidan let go of her, but she didn't fall. Heidi felt like she was floating in the air in front of him. He cupped her face with both hands, closed his eyes as she did too. His breath tickled her lips, making the wait almost unbearable, but she didn't stir.

"All right, missy," A voice shouted, dragging her painfully out of her fantasy just as it was about to hit its climax.

Heidi opened her eyes to find the same man with the

swallows standing in the doorway.

"I need you to tell me who this 'Fight4Independence' person really is."

One of his silent minions dragged a chair into the cell, the bare metal of its legs scraping against the concrete floor, making the hairs on the back of Heidi's neck stand up.

"Did you hear me? Who is 'Fight4Independence'?" The man repeated.

Crap. "I don't know the guy, okay? I just met him online," she tried to explain, but something told her, a vague answer like that wasn't going to satisfy this guy...

CHAPTER TEN

Aidan entered the office bright and early in the morning, only to find it empty. *Where was everyone?*

The clean coffee cup on Heidi's desk was dry, unused. Aidan wondered whether to go upstairs to see if she was still in bed... But that would have been too creepy, so he decided against it.

He made a quick call to Jamie instead, who picked up just when Aidan was about to give up.

"Hello?"

"Jamie. I'm back." Aidan sat down at his desk, and impatiently tapped his fingers against the already worn surface.

"Great timing, Heidi has made some progress while you were away." Jamie sounded uncharacteristically excited, especially considering the time.

"Has she? She's not here."

A crackle interrupted the awkward silence.

"She's not upstairs, either?" Jamie asked at last. His tone had changed, gone was his excitement, instead it had been replaced by... concern?

Aidan's chest tightened, and a feeling of dread came over him. He rushed to the door, up the stairs and into the room where Heidi's scent lingered the strongest. Her bed looked unused, the pillow was still fluffed up and her duvet was neatly folded and placed at the foot-end of the mattress.

"Goddammit, Jamie!" Aidan shouted into the phone. "She hasn't been here all night!"

"I... Shit. I'm coming in." Jamie hung up and Aidan

stood helplessly in the center of her room, phone still in hand. His bear wanted to come out, roar in anger and tear up the place. Where was she? Why hadn't she come home?

She had looked strong enough, Aidan had no doubt she would have been a good fighter, but the city could be a dangerous place for a lone shifter. They had files filled with names downstairs of shifters at least as capable, if not more so, who had disappeared without a trace. The last thing Aidan wanted was to have to add her name to one of the files. He wouldn't be able to stand it.

Aidan paced around the room, trying his best to control his breathing and suppress the urge to shift. After regaining a little bit of focus, he rushed back downstairs and powered up Heidi's computer in an attempt to find out what she had been working on.

Before Jamie even turned up, Aidan had read through various messages between what he assumed was Heidi's ID on the message board, and some of the regular members. They had been very chatty, much more so than they had been with him when he first joined.

"What the fuck where you thinking?" Aidan shouted, as soon as Jamie finally came through the door. "She hasn't been here a week and you let her meet with these people? She wasn't ready!"

"Watch your tone!" Jamie responded. "She seemed capable enough, and the job was simple: go meet a couple of people for drinks in a public place. Nothing more than that. Perhaps she's just hungover and..."

"I'll use whatever tone I see fit!" Aidan slammed his fist down on the desk, making it shake dangerously in the process. "She hasn't even slept in her bed! Whatever happened last night, she never made it out of there."

"Don't talk to me like it wasn't my call to make. In case you forgot, I'm the team leader. And you weren't even around!" Jamie responded.

Aidan took a couple of deep breaths and tried to control the rage that had bubbled up into his chest. He balled his fists and released them a few times, but he couldn't calm down. Jamie was right, though. Aidan had gone off on his own before even training Heidi properly. He'd had good reason to, of course, but still... How could he not feel responsible for what had happened?

"Okay, let's think about this. The last thing the Alliance needs right now is to make enemies of the Wolves of Rannoch." Jamie slowly wandered over to his desk and sat down and rested his head on his hands.

"What?" Aidan looked up again in confusion.

"Rannoch. That's where she's from."

"What the- You're telling me she's wolf?" Aidan couldn't believe his ears. This was a disaster. The woman fate had selected for him was gone. In his haste to run after ghosts from his past, he hadn't even realized the most basic details about her. He hadn't noticed she was a completely different species, and from Rannoch, no less!

He'd heard about that place, a secretive community of wolves living deep in the woods, far removed from human society. She wouldn't know the first thing about how the world worked, and probably jumped head-first into a dangerous situation with the bloody Sons of Domnall! He should have known. This was all his fault.

"Jesus Christ, Jamie. Would it have hurt you to let me know?" Aidan asked at last.

"You already weren't thrilled about her coming here, it seemed unnecessary to complicate matters further. Plus I figured you'd have noticed from her scent."

"Her scent..." Aidan shook his head. "How the fuck do I know what a wolf smells like? Fuck."

"Anyway, enough of this. Rather than continue to

blame each other, let's figure out how to fix this," Jamie suggested. He looked terrified, as though there was something else he wasn't sharing, but Aidan decided to let it go for now.

Perhaps there was still time to sort this out. The one thing he did know was that he couldn't trust Jamie with this, not fully, anyway. And if by chance Lee Campbell was involved in Heidi's disappearance as well, Aidan really needed help he could rely on to ensure he'd get the chance to capture the man himself. There was only one other person he would entrust Heidi's life with: Derek.

———◆———

By the time evening came around, Jamie had pulled fellow Alliance team member Kyle back from his vacation, and Aidan had managed to get in touch with Derek, who was on his way as well.

The office was buzzing with activity, and eerily quiet at the same time. All three of them - Aidan, Jamie, and Kyle, were each completely absorbed in their work, so they barely spoke to one another.

"I've got it!" Kyle finally broke the silence.

Aidan looked up, his eyes burning from staring at his screen for so long.

"What is it?" Jamie asked, who had gotten up to take a look at what Kyle had found.

"I've managed to hack into the phone company's server." Kyle pointed at his screen. "There. That's the cell tower Heidi was connected to when her phone went dead."

"All right..." Aidan rolled his chair up to Kyle's desk and took a look. It was just a number, a code, it might as well have been Greek to him.

"So cross-referencing the tower ID, with the grid, here," Kyle opened another screen, and showed his two colleagues a map of Edinburgh, which was divided into zones with equally confusing looking numbers in them. "It seems Heidi was roughly in this area." Kyle circled one of the zones with his index finger.

"Okay, well… that's something." Aidan scratched his head. "Jamie, you said she was going to meet people for drinks. A public place, a pub?"

"Yeah, a pub."

"How many pubs are in that area, there?" Aidan braced himself for the answer. This city - as well as most of the country - actually, was famous for its numerous drinking establishments.

"Let's see…" Kyle clicked a few buttons, and superimposed another map over the grid he'd looked at earlier. "About… thirty?"

"Thirty." Jamie let out a dejected sigh. "We don't have enough people to canvas thirty pubs in time to figure out where she went. Not without drawing attention to ourselves anyway."

"Perhaps we don't have to… What else do we know about these people? If they've taken Heidi at the meeting, they would have done it somewhere where they felt comfortable. Somewhere, where nobody would have called the police on them… They're nationalists, right? Separatists. How many of these pubs are independent, not owned by large breweries - especially not English breweries?"

"About half are free houses, not tied to any brewery."

"How else can we narrow this down? How about location? It's unlikely Heidi would have been taken from a pub that is in full view of a main road…"

"That leaves us with five. Five unaffiliated pubs that are set back from main roads." Kyle sat back, crossing his arms. "That's not half bad. Good thinking there, Aidan!"

The printer in the corner purred into action, and soon spat out a list with all the addresses. Jamie got up to retrieve it, read through it, and handed it to Aidan.

"Let's go, then. No time to waste."

————— ◆ —————

The first two pubs on the list didn't feel right to Aidan. He couldn't catch a whiff of Heidi's scent there either, so they quickly moved on to number three.

After picking up his brother, Derek, on the way, they parked up a few buildings down and walked up to the third pub. There was a Scotland flag in the window, and the place had a particular vibe to it that made Aidan suspicious.

"This could be the one," he remarked.

Jamie, next to him, nodded. "Very private, service alley leading to the back. I agree."

They decided to split up, with Jamie heading inside to look for clues there, and Aidan exploring said alley, while Derek went back to the car to keep an eye on the surrounding area. Aidan had barely made it to the back of the building, before he found what he'd been looking for.

Right next to a stack of piled up garbage bags, was unmistakable proof that they had come to the right place. A discarded hair band, a couple of strawberry blond hairs still attached to it. He picked it up and immediately caught Heidi's scent. She'd been here.

He made a quick call to Derek, telling him this was the place and to stay put. Then he decided to head inside to join Jamie, who had taken a seat at the bar.

Inside the dimly lit establishment, Aidan immediately saw that the crowd looked right too. The clientele was overwhelmingly male, working class, a lot of tightly cropped or shaved heads around the place. They fit the profile down to the combat boots and occasional nationalist tattoos. And they were all were staring at him.

Actually, both Aidan and Jamie stood out like sore thumbs. Considering how built they were, of course, it would take a lot more than wearing your hair the wrong way for any of these people to confront the two bears. After a quick greeting, they ordered whatever was on tap and immediately started commenting on the football playing on the flat screen overhead like they came here all the time.

All the heads they'd turned initially looked away again. A decent knowledge of the local sports scene was apparently enough to appease the crowd.

Although Aidan knew that time was of the essence if they wanted to get Heidi back in one piece, he also knew that patience and stealth were called for here. By the third round, they'd gotten a few of the regulars involved in an in-depth discussion about coaching decisions and seemingly blended in.

It was then that a familiar face walked in the front door and ordered a scotch. It was the younger guy from the park.

Aidan subtly signaled to Jamie that he was their man, then sent a quick text message to Derek in the car as well:

Found our guy. We'll follow him when he leaves, and once we get there, keep Jamie out of my way.

The two bears watched him from the corners of their eyes. As soon as he left, they'd be on his tail, and hopefully he'd lead them right to where Heidi was being held.

CHAPTER ELEVEN

"Answer me! How do you know 'Fight4Independence'?" The man shouted again, while his two younger partners stood silently behind him, their arms folded.

Heidi flinched with every outburst of his. Not because she was scared of him, per se. She was more terrified that if he did anything more than just raise his voice at her, she couldn't fight the urge to shift anymore. In her current state, hungry and mentally as well as physically exhausted, she'd be able to take on one, maybe two of her captors, but only if they weren't armed. If any of them had guns, she'd be down in no time.

"I told you, I don't know him in person, we met on the Internet," Heidi repeated herself for the umpteenth time.

"Why did you try to join us? Who do you work for?"

"Nobody! I just agree with your philosophy and wanted in on the action!" Heidi covered her face with her hands and tried to focus on deep, even breaths. Hyperventilating wasn't going to do anyone any good.

She had no idea how long she'd been locked up, and the hunger pangs that had been coming and going for what felt like hours were making a painful return. How much more of this would she be able to take? Like most animals, her wolf side couldn't stand being trapped.

"If you won't talk willingly, I'm going to have to find a way to make you..."

Heidi looked up to find the two silent henchmen taking a few steps in her direction. This was bad. She could feel a familiar itch develop in the pit of her stomach. Once they were on her, she wouldn't be able to control her body's urge to protect itself.

She closed her eyes again. *Come on, Aidan, if you're looking for me at all, now would be the time to find this place...* Just as she'd completed her thought her sensitive hearing picked up a disturbance elsewhere in the building. It was too faint to make out what it really was, but it sounded out of the ordinary.

Was she starting to lose her mind? Was her imagination playing tricks on her?

The noises - footsteps, the occasional thump and scream - came closer and closer, until she could pick up on actual words.

"Where is she?" someone who sounded suspiciously like Aidan demanded.

"Who?" Another voice retorted.

"Stop messing me about, where's the girl?"

Heidi swallowed her concerns, as well as her fatigue. When she opened her eyes and stared right at her main captor, she was back in control and revitalized.

"You might want to call back your goons," she warned, keeping her voice steady and low.

"Oh yeah? Why is that, lassie?" he taunted.

"They lay a finger on me, and..."

"And?"

Heidi felt her eyes burn up as she looked around the room. Even the most casual observer would clearly be able to see them glow in the dark. One of the younger men flinched back, but the other one, and the guy in charge didn't react at all. This wasn't the first time they'd seen a shifter readying for a fight.

"I knew it," he said, a subtle smile playing on his lips. "There was something not right about you. We're done here. Take care of her."

His two underlings exchanged a quick glance, and then

approached her again. They weren't going to deal with her using just their bare hands, though. This time, one reached around, retrieving something from his belt. A hunting knife.

Heidi held her breath and waited for them to come closer. If all they had were knives, she'd be fine. This is what she had trained for. Guns, however...

The footsteps reached outside the door, followed by a loud crash of metal against metal. The wooden frame splintered, and the reinforced door flew open, revealing a slightly red-faced Aidan, holding a hand-held steel battering ram.

Are you okay? His eyes seemed to ask as they exchanged a quick look. Heidi responded with only a smile. Her heart fluttered at the sight of him. He had come to free her. *Her hero.*

Her three captors turned to face this new threat, giving Heidi the perfect opportunity to get involved in the fun. Within a split second, she'd allowed her animal side to take over. The shackles that had kept her tied to the bed fell off her much sleeker paws, as did the clothes she'd been wearing. She pounced on the first person that came her way.

There was no room in her mind for moderation, for keeping things clean. Her sharp teeth tore through flesh and crunched bone, until her prey was left in a puddle on the floor, whimpering in pain.

The other two looked back at her in horror, but didn't have time to dwell on what had just happened, because Aidan was coming at them with the steel ram he'd just used on the door. The young one flew back against the wall at the far end of the cell, leaving only the senior one still in one piece.

That's when things calmed down very suddenly.

"Lee Campbell, I presume… We have some unfinished business," Aidan said in a low voice.

"I'd been wondering when you'd turn up."

Despite adrenaline still coursing through her veins, Heidi decided to sit down right in between the two incapacitated men to just observe. *How did these two know each other?* This must have been one of the men Aidan had seen at the park, the one he said he'd recognized.

"Then you know what this is about?" Aidan asked.

"I got a call from a friend in Portree the other day…"

Aidan nodded, as if that explained everything.

The other henchman, whom Aidan had thrown all the way across the room, groaned as he tried to reach for the hunting knife that was lying on the floor mere feet away from him. Heidi quickly intervened, and with a growl kicked the knife out of his reach. *Watch yourself or you'll get mauled like your friend,* she thought.

"Back in 1999, Skye. Your parents," the man Aidan had identified as Lee Campbell said.

"That's right." Aidan placed his hand on Lee's shoulder and shoved him backwards across the room, until he reached the bed. As Lee sat, Aidan grabbed the steel chair and positioned himself across from him. "Why?"

"Why…" Lee let out a chuckle. "Why do bad things happen to good people? Why is life so unfair?"

"If your organization killed them simply for what they were, then why let me and my brother live?"

Heidi held her breath. This man had killed Aidan's parents? That was it, Aidan's deep, dark secret. That was why he was so focused on his work with the Alliance.

She thought of her own parents, and felt her earlier rage flare up again on Aidan's behalf. Hidden underneath the controlled exterior, Heidi saw signs that Aidan was struggling with his emotions as well. The animal inside him wanted revenge, while his human side needed answers. Every muscle in Aidan's body had tensed up. His heartbeat was racing, she could hear it clearly from across the room.

"For who they were? No, son, they didn't die for who they were, but for *where* they were and *when*."

Aidan frowned. "What are you saying?"

"Wrong place, wrong time. Just bad luck. A coincidence," Lee clarified, and shrugged. "They saw something they shouldn't have. Believe me, had I known there was more to them than that, you wouldn't be here right now."

Heidi couldn't believe her ears. As slick and organized as all of her people thought the Sons of Domnall were, they seemed to be a rather confused bunch. Killing shifters without knowing they were shifters, just because they couldn't keep their shenanigans secret without being overseen by random bystanders. Wow.

Aidan gave her a knowing look, like he could read her mind.

Kill him, he deserves to die, Heidi thought. Aidan subtly shook his head. *Not yet.*

"I've thought about this moment for years. Fifteen years, to be exact. What I'd do to you once I found you." Aidan folded his arms and stared at Lee, who looked unusually content for someone who had just been captured by the enemy.

"Do what you must, sonny."

"I could kill you right now, but what good would that do anyone? No. I think you'll be of more use alive..."

Aidan got up and retrieved a pair of handcuffs from his pocket. Lee didn't struggle, he barely even reacted when Aidan cuffed him with his hands behind his back. The entire scene was surreal, and for a moment, Heidi wondered if she had perhaps passed out due to hunger and was just imagining everything.

"Is this the guy?" another man said as he burst into the room. The similarities between Aidan and him were uncanny, even if he did look like a wilder, more feral version of him. Scruffy beard and longer hair, but their body structure and even their walks were alike. They had to be related, brothers perhaps.

"Derek. Stand down," Aidan warned him, placing his hand against his chest.

Behind Derek, Jamie came into view, wiping his brow with the back of his hand. "What's the status here?"

"Heidi is secure. One guy in critical condition," Aidan glanced at the bleeding man Heidi had sharpened her teeth on earlier. "Another with a few bruises and this one here, Lee Campbell, senior Sons of Domnall member. Captured."

"All right. We've had a few runners, half a dozen or so, two casualties, three prisoners who are somewhat unharmed," Jamie responded.

Holy crap, casualties?! Heidi had been aware of the risks of this work, but it was still surreal hearing her boss report actual deaths in such a matter-of-fact tone. The Alliance was a relatively small set-up, especially in Edinburgh, but they clearly knew how to get their hands dirty.

"You," Jamie addressed Heidi directly now. "You can't go out like this."

Heidi instinctively flinched at his strict tone, and hated herself for it immediately. Jamie was her boss, but he wasn't her alpha.

"Relax, she's not going to," Aidan butted in.

"Fine. Let's get out of here before anyone else sees us. Kyle has already brought the van around." Jamie grabbed Lee Campbell by the arm and dragged him out of the room. Behind him, Derek paused for a moment, but then made his exit as well, stopping only to drag out both the incapacitated henchmen out by their arms. Finally, Aidan and Heidi were on their own.

"You, umm... I should give you some privacy," Aidan mumbled, while watching Heidi pick up her clothes between her teeth. He turned around and headed for the door as well. Heidi channeled all her energy into one final instant shift and followed Aidan to the door, placing her hand on his shoulder.

"Wait."

He paused, allowing Heidi to catch up properly and face him. She didn't care that she was butt naked. She didn't care that they were surrounded by filth. All she cared about was that she was finally reunited with the man she knew she was going to spend the rest of her life with.

She wrapped her arms around his neck, and pressed her lips against his.

If he was surprised at her sudden change of heart, he didn't show it. Instead, he held her tightly in his arms, and responded to her kisses with an urgency that matched her own. His touch was electric, and his kisses...

Tears started to stream down her face.

"I thought I'd die in here. That I'd never see you again," Heidi whispered.

"Impossible. I wouldn't have let that happen," Aidan responded.

He cupped her face, just like he had done before in her dreams, and gazed into her eyes.

She could see hidden depths in his brown eyes that hadn't been there before. Or perhaps she never actually had allowed herself to look.

In the short time she'd known him, he'd seemed totally independent. She had never been really sure he felt their connection as intensely has she had, but there in his eyes, she found a different Aidan. The teenager who had lost both his parents to a stupid coincidence, who all of a sudden was forced to grow up. She saw Aidan, the man, who felt that he could never truly rely on anyone but himself. That's why he hadn't told Jamie the truth about why he had to take off for a couple of days. Who could be charming if he wanted to be, but had never let anyone come too close.

Until now.

"You have very green eyes, has anyone ever told you that?" Aidan remarked.

Heidi laughed, then tiptoed and kissed him again. "What happens now?" she asked.

Aidan stole a glance down at her naked chest and gave her another one of those sexy, brooding looks he'd given her at the pub on her first night. "How about you cover up and we get out of here?"

"What about the prisoners? And Jamie and all?" Heidi asked.

"They're not going anywhere. You've been locked in here for over a day, if that's not deserving of a little time off, I don't know what is."

Heidi smiled. "Fair enough. Before anything else, I could murder another one of those fish platters from that pub."

"What, raw man flesh didn't sate your appetite?" Aidan teased.

"Nah, I prefer my meat cooked." Heidi released Aidan's neck, and walked back across the cell to get her clothes, all the while feeling his intense stare on her naked body. Oh, she could definitely use some time off, but had a feeling it wouldn't involve much relaxation.

CHAPTER TWELVE

Aidan hadn't been able to keep his eyes off Heidi while she got dressed inside her cell. He hadn't been willing to let go of her hand as they walked out of the dark, damp warehouse where she'd been locked up. He had had a taste of her lips, and both man and bear needed more of the same.

When he'd seen her shift and attack one of her captors, he had to admit to himself he'd been impressed. She had held up remarkably well in captivity. When faced with four blank walls and no way out, it was easy to lose hope and lash out. She had kept her cool though, and waited for the right moment to attack. When she did, it had been a glorious display of the force of nature. Cruel, efficient, beautiful.

As much as he hated him for it, Jamie had been right. Heidi was capable. A great addition to the team and the Alliance overall. If only he didn't feel so goddamn protective of her.

The connection between the two of them hadn't been as clear as he'd heard about in other fated couples, but every time they were in the same room together, their bond seemed to grow stronger. When he'd just reached the hideout, he could feel her presence. He knew she was alive, and scared.

When he'd found her, he could even hear glimpses of her thoughts. He was used to keeping secrets, mostly from Jamie, but even from Derek. Still, it seemed nice to have someone in his life who would always know what he was thinking. Someone who would understand him no matter what.

Although she'd said she wanted to return to the same place where they'd eaten on her first night in town, they didn't quite make it there. The first kebab shop on the way proved too tempting. Grilled meat could do that to a person, especially one who was also a wolf.

Aidan watched her eat, no, inhale the food. The color returned to her cheeks, making her look all the more tempting.

"What?" Heidi looked up from the now empty wrapper that had only moments earlier contained a lamb wrap.

"Nothing." Aidan grinned and made no attempt to look away.

"No, seriously. What are you staring at?"

"I love watching you eat. Wait, that sounds creepy, doesn't it?"

"You ought to work on your lines, sweetheart. *Creepy* is an understatement." Heidi grinned back at him.

"Still hungry?" Aidan teased.

"You're impossible. And no, I think I'm done," Heidi responded.

Aidan got up to pay for the food, when his phone buzzed. Jamie. He'd seen Aidan's message stating that he was taking Heidi home for some much needed rest and agreed. They wouldn't be expected back at the office until the next morning.

"Who was that?" Heidi asked when Aidan shoved his phone back into his pocket.

"The boss. Time off approved."

"Gee, I wonder how we will pass the time?" Heidi blinked at Aidan quasi-innocently.

"I have a few ideas." Aidan offered her his hand and off they went, straight to his place.

———— ♦ ————

"Wow, this is nice!" Heidi remarked, after Aidan had unlocked the front door and stepped aside to let her enter first.

"Welcome to my humble abode." Aidan gestured around the cozy living room. "Make yourself at home."

"Oh, I intend to. I've had enough of cold, musty cells for a while. And that includes the bloody Alliance building with what you people so generously refer to as "rooms" upstairs."

Aidan let out a laugh. "Oh, that. Yeah... I lasted one night when I first arrived. Went house hunting the very next day."

Heidi took off her coat and placed it over the backrest of the sofa. Then she turned to face Aidan again.

"So, where were we earlier?" she asked in a low, seductive voice.

Her question unleashed a whole load of explicit thoughts in his mind. She was here with him, and willing. Why wait? Why hold back any longer?

Rather than voice his desires, he picked her up in one swift move and carried her through the living room, down the hall and into his bedroom. She giggled the entire way, and once on her back in his bed, looked up at him with those big, bright green eyes of hers until he could resist no more.

He got up onto the bed on all fours and kissed her again. And again, until both their lips got sore.

As her hands roamed over his back, setting him alight from within, he raised himself up again and moved down lower, grabbing the collar of her t-shirt between his teeth. He pulled, hard, until the fabric gave way with a loud tear.

The glimpse he'd gotten earlier after she'd shifted back was still burning in his mind, and he couldn't wait to get her back to her natural state. After ridding her of her top entirely, as well as her bra, he tore her jeans off her using just his hands.

Heidi was also getting into the swing of things and started clawing at his clothes. Within moments, they were both naked.

She really was a beautiful woman. Tall, with long, shapely legs, and endless curves in all the right places. Some men liked their women petite and slim, but Aidan was not one of them; he liked to play rough, and that was only possible with someone who could match his passion.

In Heidi, he'd found everything he could ever hope for. As he started to explore her soft, silky skin with his fingertips and lips - occasionally his teeth - the looks she gave him betrayed that gentle love-making was the last thing on her mind either.

Their union would be spectacular, that much was certain.

But first, he needed to taste her. The scent of her arousal hung heavy in the air, intoxicating him completely. His bear roared with excitement, and tried to push him to hurry up with the foreplay, and get on to the main course already, but he chose to resist just a little bit longer.

Heidi had other ideas though, and wrapped her fingers tightly around his thick shaft. "I need you. Oh God, I need you so badly," she breathed.

As she started to pump him, slowly at first, she never once broke eye contact.

Aidan closed his eyes, and tried to fight the building tension within him. He wouldn't cum. Not yet. Oh, hell!

He opened his eyes again and grabbed her wrists tightly, forcing her arms up above her head. No more touching. If she wanted him, she could have him. Right now, and when they were done, they would go again, and again, until she'd be too tired to give him that look. The one she was giving him right now.

This stare, it wasn't a request, it was a command. She demanded that he take her.

He couldn't hold off any longer and positioned himself between her thighs, pressing the head of his cock against her tight entrance. She was slick for him. Ready. But nice girls from Rannoch didn't go around fucking boys in their spare time. He didn't need to ask to know that he was her first. It was painfully obvious.

Heidi shut her eyes when he lowered himself on top of her, and her body finally made way for him.

She cried out, but when she looked at him again he could see that it wasn't a cry of pain.

He started off slow, rocking his hips into her, until he felt her relax. This was new for her, and he felt grateful - no, he felt proud to be her first. They would remember this moment forever.

As he settled into a more comfortable rhythm, her body started to react. Each thrust of his she met, her moans getting louder and louder. He loosened his grip on her wrists and her arms wrapped around his neck, clutching him tighter against her naked chest.

Their excitement turned more and more feverish. He focused on the rhythm, the in and out. Her body twitching and bucking upward in waves.

He felt her heat grow, her reactions turn more skittish and involuntary. She was heading up the cliff, and he was going to push her over the summit.

Heidi's hands twitched, fingernails dug hard into Aidan's back. It didn't bother him – if anything, it got him more excited. She turned rigid and groaned loudly, while dragging her hand down across his shoulder blade. The metallic scent of blood hung in the air, but rather than slow, Aidan sped up.

The sting on his back made his arousal grow. He plunged into her faster and faster, as she helplessly lay on her back panting through the remainder of her orgasm.

He finally reached the limits of his own control and jumped off that cliff after her, filling her with his hot seed, while sweet pleasure washed over him, paralyzing every one of his muscles. The room had suddenly turned so very quiet, while they both tried to catch their breath.

Neither of them stirred until Heidi started to nibble on the side of his neck.

"That was amazing. I never expected it to be *that* amazing."

Aidan smiled as he lifted himself off her. Without saying a word, he gathered her up in his arms and carried her into the spacious bathroom for round two. They could both use a hot shower after all they'd been through today, and he'd make sure to clean her out properly with his tongue... Virgin no more, he was intent on showing Heidi just how much more amazing stuff they could do to one another. After all, she was his now, and he was hers.

———— ◆ ————

Aidan stole a glance at the sleeping beauty beside him. Yes, she was a wolf, and he was a bear, and that complicated matters significantly. They would have an uphill battle ahead. But looking at her now, blissfully asleep on his pillow, he felt like none of that mattered.

The Alliance didn't approve of inter-species relationships. No doubt Heidi's parents would have a fit if they found out. But was it any of their business, really? She had come to him, she had accepted him. Once they made it official, what could anyone do about it?

Bears didn't have a lot of laws and traditions, but one that was carved in stone was that you didn't mess with a bear's mate. Wolf society was much more regimented and bound by a whole barrage of rules, but in this respect their cultures intersected: the bond between mates was considered sacred.

Plus, if it was good enough for Derek and Clarice, whose bond had been finalized only moments before he had called Derek away, it would be good enough for Heidi and him.

Aidan carefully lifted Heidi's arm off his chest and got up. There, inside the top drawer of the bedside table next to him, he already had everything they would need... Aidan retrieved the sealed envelope he had carried home from McMillan Farm. Its contents clanged together. The jingling sound was muffled by the thick parchment surrounding it, but he could still hear it.

"What are you doing?" Heidi said behind him, and rested her hand on his bare back.

Aidan turned around, envelope still in hand. "Here," he said. "Open it." Although he knew this was the right way of handling things, he was still anxious about how she would react. Was it too soon?

Heidi rubbed her eyes and sat up straight in the bed. Then she took the envelope from him and slipped her finger underneath the lip, levering the red wax seal off the paper underneath. She held her breath and looked inside.

"Oh! Are these what I think they are?" she whispered.

"These belonged to my parents," Aidan said. "Since they were designed for bears, yours may not fit quite right, but I'm sure we'll work something out."

Heidi took out the smaller of the two rings, and held it

up to get a better look at it. "It's gorgeous."

"As are you." Aidan took a deep breath. "So, what do you say? Will you be mine forever, as I'll be yours?"

She blinked a few times, yet failed to hide the tears collecting in the corner of her eyes. "Of course. I love you."

"I love you, too."

EPILOGUE

"Morning," Jamie said as he walked into the office, shaking off his umbrella and leaving it in a bucket in the corner.

Aidan and Heidi exchanged a quick look before responding. *He wouldn't be able to tell what's going on, would he?* Heidi wondered, while instinctively reaching for the ring hanging from a chain around her neck. His mother's ring. They'd showered before coming in, but still she felt like the whole world would be able to smell the sex on them. And she'd heard it said that something happened to couples after they were fully mated. That other people would be able to tell.

No way, Aidan responded. *We've been careful.* His hand was resting on his pocket where she knew he'd kept his ring. Maybe one day they'd feel safe enough to wear them openly, but not yet.

Heidi suppressed a smile. It was nice, having Aidan in her head. Where earlier she'd been able to catch only glimpses of his mood, it was reassuring being able to communicate with him, without even saying a word out loud.

"So where are we with the prisoners?" Jamie asked.

"They're secure in the basement. We've been questioning them one by one and so far none of them are in a mood to talk," Aidan said.

"How about you, well rested?" Jamie asked Heidi.

"Yeah. Fine. Ready to get back to work." Heidi smiled at him, let go of her chain, then looked back down at her computer screen.

"Good. Carry on." Jamie sighed and started on his

usual morning routine, walking over to the coffee maker, and shoveling spoonful after spoonful of sugar into his cup, before pouring the black liquid over it.

"Aidan, I want you to bring in your informant, what was her name? Alison." Jamie stirred his coffee and turned around while taking the first, careful sip.

"Do you think that's wise? Shouldn't I meet her out in public, as usual?" Aidan asked.

Heidi pretended not to listen, but stole a glance in Aidan's direction anyway. *Who was this Alison person?*

Our informant. Human, Aidan responded.

"She's been instrumental in identifying the websites. Don't you trust her?" Jamie asked.

"I suppose…"

"Well then perhaps it's time to question her properly, both of us, capture it on video." Jamie took another loud sip, then walked over to his desk and sat down with a loud creak.

"It's your call."

"Bring her in."

Aidan leaned forward, grabbing his phone off his desk and scrolling through his address book.

"Oh, where's your brother... Derek, was it?" Jamie asked. "I didn't have the chance to thank him for his help yesterday."

"Derek left bright and early."

Of course he did, Heidi thought. *Aidan had basically called the poor guy away from his honeymoon to help out with her rescue.*

"That's a shame. Nice guy. We could've used him on the team..."

"Uhuh," Aidan responded, while playing with his phone again.

Jamie sat back and looked around the office, pausing on both of their faces for a bit too long. The extra attention made Heidi nervous, but she resisted the urge to fidget with her chain again.

"Guys. It's okay, you know..." Jamie started, "It may be controversial in some circles, but you have nothing to worry about here."

Heidi tried to swallow her worries, and looked up at him as coolly as she could manage. "Worry about what?"

"Right." Jamie grinned and diverted his attention to his computer, which had just switched on. "Worry about what, indeed... Excuse me for a moment, I am going to pay a little visit to our guests downstairs."

While Jamie gathered up some notes and a pen, along with his half-empty cup of coffee, Heidi tried her best to remain calm.

As soon as he was out the door, she pulled her chair across the office, right next to Aidan's.

"He knows! Despite being careful, he still knows!" She couldn't believe it. Aidan was right, they *had* been careful. So how did he figure it out?

"I'm not surprised. He's been doing this kind of work for a long time. Good instincts," Aidan responded.

"Now what?"

"Nothing. We can't very well undo what has happened. Neither can we force him to forget."

"But the way you act around the guy, like you don't trust him. Are you sure he won't rat us out?" Heidi asked.

"I don't think he would."

"So why didn't you tell him why you were really driving up to Skye?" Heidi insisted. "Why keep secrets?"

"Because it was none of his business. And because Jamie Abbott isn't his real name. I've only been able to uncover records for *one* Jamie Abbott living in Scotland, and he's been dead ten years."

Heidi was speechless. Jamie wasn't who he said he was?

That was huge, and strangely, Aidan seemed quite calm about the entire affair.

"I don't understand. Either we're all on the same side, or we're not."

"I've found nothing to suggest he's disloyal to the cause, all I know is that for some reason or other he's chosen to live under an alias. Trust me. Things will be fine. He won't tell a soul." Aidan placed his hand on Heidi's shoulder and gave it a gentle squeeze.

"Fine. I trust you." Heidi closed her eyes and rested her head against Aidan's hand. Amazing, how such a simple gesture could put her mind at ease. She *did* trust him, and her own instincts were usually right about people too. During their time working together, she'd never felt unsafe around Jamie. He had his secrets, but then that might well be a bear thing, because Aidan had his too. Maybe one day, with Aidan's help, she'd understand why bears were so secretive...

"What do you say, we head downstairs to observe Jamie as he has a go questioning the prisoners? We might learn something." Aidan got up and offered her his hand.

"Sure." Heidi accepted his gesture, and together they left the office, ready to embark on whatever new adventures might lie ahead.

***

ABOUT THE AUTHOR

Dear Reader,

Thanks for reading Scottish Werebear: Dangerous Business, Book 2 in the Scottish Werebears Series. Although this is my first published series, I'm not new to writing in general. In fact, my mom still tells me to this day about how I would make up stories, and attempt to record them in my clumsy, shaky handwriting from the moment I learned to read and write. From there I went on to write fan fiction and other stuff meant for my own eyes only.

I've always enjoyed stories of the paranormal. Vampires, shape shifters, witches and magic, all featured in the books I loved the most, even when I was still growing up. But it wasn't until much later that I got into romance. One of the first writers (a self-published author just like me!) I came across was Tina Folsom, via her Scanguards Vampire series. I was hooked. From there I went on to read more paranormal romance until I found a new favorite kind of hero: bear shifters, like the kind written by Milly Taiden, Zoe Chant, and T.S. Joyce. What I love about bears is how they can be all strong and independent, a bit reclusive, and almost grumpy, but they always end up having a heart of gold (plus they tend to know their food, and we all know that a man who can cook is doubly sexy). All that (except for the shifting into a powerful bear) almost exactly describes the sort of man I ended up falling for and marrying in real life, so it's no surprise that this is what I started my publishing career with.

To find out more, check:
LoreleiMoone.com (And why not sign up for the newsletter to be the first to find out about new releases.)

You can also get in touch with me via Facebook (search for Lorelei Moone), or email at info@loreleimoone.com

I also write contemporary romance as L. Moone. If that's something you're interested in, you can take a look at LMoone.com.

x Lorelei